THE GREAT WALL
OF CHINA

THE GREAT WALL
OF CHINA

Stories and Reflections

FRANZ KAFKA

Translated by Willa and Edwin Muir

SCHOCKEN BOOKS · NEW YORK

First SCHOCKEN PAPERBACK edition 1970

10 9 8 7 6   79 80 81 82

Copyright 1936, 1937 by Heinr. Mercy Sohn, Prague
Copyright 1946 by Schocken Books Inc.

Library of Congress Catalog Card No. 46-8109

Printed in the United States of America

CONTENTS

INVESTIGATIONS
OF A DOG

HOW MUCH my life has changed, and yet how unchanged it has remained at bottom! When I think back and recall the time when I was still a member of the canine community, sharing in all its preoccupations, a dog among dogs, I find on closer examination that from the very beginning I sensed some discrepancy, some little maladjustment, causing a slight feeling of discomfort which not even the most decorous public functions could eliminate; more, that sometimes, no, not sometimes, but very often, the mere look of some fellow dog of my own circle that I was fond of, the mere look of him, as if I had just caught it for the first time, would fill me with helpless embarrassment and fear, even with despair. I tried to quiet my apprehensions as best I could; friends, to whom I divulged them, helped me; more peaceful times came—times, it is true, in which these sudden surprises were not lacking, but in which they were accepted with more philosophy, fitted into my life with more philosophy, inducing a certain melancholy and lethargy, it may be, but nevertheless allowing me to carry on as a somewhat cold, reserved, shy, and calculating, but all things considered normal enough dog. How, indeed, without these breathing spells, could I have reached the age that I enjoy at present; how could I have fought my way

1

through to the serenity with which I contemplate the terrors of youth and endure the terrors of age; how could I have come to the point where I am able to draw the consequences of my admittedly unhappy, or, to put it more moderately, not very happy disposition, and live almost entirely in accordance with them? Solitary and withdrawn, with nothing to occupy me save my hopeless but, as far as I am concerned, indispensable little investigations, that is how I live; yet in my distant isolation I have not lost sight of my people, news often penetrates to me, and now and then I even let news of myself reach them. The others treat me with respect but do not understand my way of life; yet they bear me no grudge, and even young dogs whom I sometimes see passing in the distance, a new generation of whose childhood I have only a vague memory, do not deny me a reverential greeting.

For it must not be assumed that, for all my peculiarities, which lie open to the day, I am so very different from the rest of my species. Indeed when I reflect on it—and I have time and disposition and capacity enough for that—I see that dogdom is in every way a marvelous institution. Apart from us dogs there are all sorts of creatures in the world, wretched, limited, dumb creatures who have no language but mechanical cries; many of us dogs study them, have given them names, try to help them, educate them, uplift them, and so on. For my part I am quite indifferent to them except when they try to disturb me, I confuse them with one another, I ignore them. But one thing is too obvious to have escaped me; namely how little inclined they are, compared with us dogs, to stick together, how silently and unfamiliarly and with what a curious hostility they pass each other by, how only the basest of interests can bind them together for a little in ostensible union, and how often these very interests give rise to hatred and conflict. Consider us dogs, on the other hand! One can safely say that we all live together in a literal heap, all of us, different as we are from one another on account of numberless and profound modifications which have arisen in the course of time. All in one heap! We are drawn to each other and nothing can prevent us from satisfying that communal impulse; all our laws and institutions, the few that I still know and the many that I have forgotten, go back to this longing for the greatest bliss we are capable of, the warm comfort of being together. But now consider the other side of the picture. No creatures to my knowledge live in such wide dispersion as we dogs, none have so many distinctions of class, of kind, of occupation, distinctions too numerous to review at a glance; we, whose one desire is to stick together—and again and again we succeed at transcendent moments in spite of everything— we above all others live so widely separated from one another, engaged in strange vocations that are often incomprehensible even to our canine neighbors, holding firmly to laws that are not those of the dog world, but are actually directed against it. How baffling these questions are, questions on which one would prefer not to touch—I understand that standpoint too, even better than my own—and yet questions to which I have completely capitulated. Why do I not do as the others: live in harmony with my people and accept in silence whatever disturbs the harmony, ignoring it as a small error in the great account, always keeping in mind the things that bind us happily together, not those that drive us again and again, as though by sheer force, out of our social circle?

I can recall an incident in my youth; I was at the time in one of those inexplicable blissful states of exaltation which everyone must have experienced as a child; I was still quite a puppy, everything pleased me, everything was my concern. I believed that great things were going on around me of which I was the leader and to which I must lend my voice, things which must be wretchedly thrown aside if I did not run for them and wag my tail for them—childish fantasies that faded with riper years. But at the time their power was very great, I was completely under their spell, and presently something actually did happen, something so extraordinary that it seemed to justify my wild expectations. In itself it was nothing very extraordinary, for I have seen many such things, and more remarkable things too, often enough since, but at the time it struck me with all the force of a first impression, one of those impressions which can never be erased and influence much of one's later conduct. I encountered, in short, a little company of dogs, or rather I did not encounter them, they appeared before me. Before that I had been running along in darkness for some time, filled with a premonition of great things—a premonition that may well have been delusive, for I always had it. I had run in darkness for a long time, up and down, blind and deaf to everything, led on by nothing but a vague desire, and now I suddenly came to a stop with the feeling that I was in the right place, and looking up saw that it was bright day, only a little hazy, and everywhere a blending and confusion of the most intoxicating smells; I greeted the morning with an uncertain barking, when—as if I had conjured them up—out of some place of darkness, to the accompaniment of terrible sounds such as I had never heard before, seven dogs stepped into the light. Had I not distinctly seen that they were dogs and that they themselves brought the sound with them—though I could not recognize how they produced it—I would have run away at once; but as it was I stayed. At that time I still knew hardly anything of the creative gift for music with which the canine race alone is endowed, it had naturally enough escaped my but slowly developing powers of observation; for though music had surrounded me as a perfectly natural and indispensable element of existence ever since I was a suckling, an element which nothing impelled me to distinguish from the rest of existence, my elders had drawn my attention to it only by such hints as were suitable for a childish understanding; all the more astonishing, then, indeed devastating, were these seven great musical artists to me. They did not speak, they

did not sing, they remained generally silent, almost deter-
minedly silent; but from the empty air they conjured music.
Everything was music, the lifting and setting down of
their feet, certain turns of the head, their running and their
standing still, the positions they took up in relation to one
another, the symmetrical patterns which they produced by
one dog setting his front paws on the back of another and
the rest following suit until the first bore the weight of
the other six, or by all lying flat on the ground and going
through complicated concerted evolutions; and none made
a false move, not even the last dog, though he was a little
unsure, did not always establish contact at once with the
others, sometimes hesitated, as it were, on the stroke of the
beat, but yet was unsure only by comparison with the
superb sureness of the others, and even if he had been
much more unsure, indeed quite unsure, would not have been
able to do any harm, the others, great masters all of them,
keeping the rhythm so unshakably. But it is too much to say
that I even saw them, that I actually even saw them. They
appeared from somewhere, I inwardly greeted them as dogs,
and although I was profoundly confused by the sounds that
accompanied them, yet they were dogs nevertheless, dogs like
you and me; I regarded them by force of habit simply as dogs
I had happened to meet on my road, and felt a wish to approach them and exchange greetings; they were quite near
too, dogs much older than me, certainly, and not of my woolly,
long-haired kind, but yet not so very alien in size and shape,
indeed quite familiar to me, for I had already seen many such
or similar dogs; but while I was still involved in these reflections the music gradually got the upper hand, literally knocked
the breath out of me and swept me far away from those actual
little dogs, and quite against my will, while I howled as if
some pain were being inflicted upon me, my mind could attend
to nothing but this blast of music which seemed to come from
all sides, from the heights, from the deeps, from everywhere,

surrounding the listener, overwhelming him, crushing him, and over his swooning body still blowing fanfares so near that they seemed far away and almost inaudible. And then a respite came, for one was already too exhausted, too annulled, too feeble to listen any longer; a respite came and I beheld again the seven little dogs carrying out their evolutions, making their leaps; I longed to shout to them in spite of their aloofness, to beg them to enlighten me, to ask them what they were doing—I was a child and believed I could ask anybody about anything—but hardly had I begun, hardly did I feel on good and familiar doggish terms with the seven, when the music started again, robbed me of my wits, whirled me around in its circles as if I myself were one of the musicians instead of being only their victim, cast me hither and thither, no matter how much I begged for mercy, and rescued me finally from its own violence by driving me into a labyrinth of wooden bars which rose around that place, though I had not noticed it before, but which now firmly caught me, kept my head pressed to the ground, and thought the music still resounded in the open space behind me, gave me a little time to get my breath back. I must admit that I was less surprised by the artistry of the seven dogs—it was incomprehensible to me, and also quite definitely beyond my capacities—than by their courage in facing so openly the music of their own making, and their power to endure it calmly without collapsing. But now from my hiding hole I saw, on looking more closely, that it was not so much coolness as the most extreme tension that characterized their performance; these limbs apparently so sure in their movements quivered at every step with a perpetual apprehensive twitching; as if rigid with despair the dogs kept their eyes fixed on one another, and their tongues, whenever the tension weakened for a moment, hung wearily from their jowls. It could not be fear of failure that agitated them so deeply; dogs that could dare and achieve such things had no need to fear that. Then why were they afraid? Who then forced them to do what they were doing? And I could no longer restrain myself, particularly as they now seemed in some incomprehensible way in need of help, and so through all the din of the music I shouted out my questions loudly and challengingly. But they—incredible! incredible!—they never replied, behaved as if I were not there. Dogs who make no reply to the greeting of other dogs are guilty of an offense against good manners which the humblest dog would never pardon any more than the greatest. Perhaps they were not dogs at all? But how should they not be dogs? Could I not actually hear on listening more closely the subdued cries with which they encouraged each other, drew each other's attention to difficulties, warned each other against errors; could I not see the last and youngest dog, to whom most of those cries were addressed, often stealing a glance at me as if he would have dearly wished to reply, but refrained because it was not allowed? But why should it not be allowed, why should the very thing which our laws unconditionally command not be allowed in this one case? I became indignant at the thought and almost forgot the music. Those dogs were violating the law. Great magicians they might be, but the law was valid for them too, I knew that quite well though I was a child. And having recognized that, I now noticed something else. They had good grounds for remaining silent, that is, assuming that they remained silent from a sense of shame. For how were they conducting themselves? Because of all the music I had not noticed it before, but they had flung away all shame, the wretched creatures were doing the very thing which is both most ridiculous and indecent in our eyes; they were walking on their hind legs. Fie on them! They were uncovering their nakedness, blatantly making a show of their nakedness: they were doing that as though it were a meritorious act, and when, obeying their better instincts for a moment, they happened to let their front paws fall, they were literally appalled as if at an error, as if Nature were an error, hastily raised their legs again, and their eyes seemed to be begging for forgiveness for having been forced to cease momentarily from their abomination. Was the world standing on its head? Where could I be? What could have happened? If only for my own sake I dared not hesitate any longer now, I dislodged myself from the tangle of bars, took one leap into the open and made towards the dogs—I, the young pupil, must be the teacher now, must make them understand what they were doing, must keep them from committing further sin. "And old dogs too! And old dogs too!" I kept on saying to myself. But scarcely was I free and only a leap or two away from the dogs, when the music again had me in its power. Perhaps in my eagerness I might even have managed to withstand it, for I knew it better now, if in the midst of all its majestic amplitude, which was terrifying, but still not inconquerable, a clear, piercing, continuous note which came without variation literally from the remotest distance—perhaps the real melody in the midst of the music—had not now rung out, forcing me to my knees. Oh, the music these dogs made almost drove me out of my senses! I could not move a step farther, I no longer wanted to instruct them; they could go on raising their front legs, committing sin and seducing others to the sin of silently regarding them; I was such a young dog —who could demand such a difficult task from me? I made myself still more insignificant than I was, I whimpered, and if the dogs had asked me now what I thought of their performance, probably I would have had not a word to say against it. Besides, it was not long before the dogs vanished with all their music and their radiance into the darkness from which they had emerged.

As I have already said, this whole episode contains nothing of much note; in the course of a long life one encounters all sorts of things which, taken from their context and seen through the eyes of a child, might well seem far more astonishing. Besides, one may, of course—in the pungent popular

phrase—have "got it all wrong," as well as everything connected with it; then it could be demonstrated that this was
simply a case where seven musicians had assembled to practice their art in the morning stillness, that a very young dog
had strayed to the place, a burdensome intruder whom they
had tried to drive away by particularly terrifying or lofty
music, unfortunately without success. He pestered them with
his questions: were they, already disturbed enough by the
mere presence of the stranger, to be expected to attend to his
distracting interruptions as well and make them worse by
responding to them? Even if the law commands us to reply
to everybody, was such a tiny stray dog in truth a somebody
worthy of the name? And perhaps they did not even understand him, for he likely enough barked his questions very indistinctly. Or perhaps they did understand him and with great
self-control answered his questions, but he, a mere puppy
unaccustomed to music, could not distinguish the answer
from the music. And as for walking on their hind legs, perhaps,
unlike other dogs, they actually used only these for walking;
if it was a sin, well, it was a sin. But they were alone, seven
friends together, an intimate gathering within their own four
walls so to speak, quite private so to speak; for one's friends,
after all, are not the public, and where the public is not
present an inquisitive little street dog is certainly not capable
of constituting it; but, granting this, is it not as if nothing
at all had happened? It is not quite so, but very nearly so,
and parents should not let their children run about so freely,
and had much better teach them to hold their tongues and
respect the aged.

If all this is admitted, then it disposes of the whole case.
But many things that are disposed of in the minds of grown-
ups are not yet settled in the minds of the young. I rushed
about, told my story, asked questions, made accusations and
investigations, tried to drag others to the place where all this
had happened, and burned to show everybody where I had

stood and where the seven had stood, and where and how they had danced and made their music; and if anyone had come with me, instead of shaking me off and laughing at me, I would probably have sacrificed my innocence and tried myself to stand on my hind legs so as to reconstruct the scene clearly. Now children are blamed for all they do, but also in the last resort forgiven for all they do. And I have preserved my childlike qualities, and in spite of that have grown to be an old dog. Well, just as at that time I kept on unceasingly discussing the foregoing incident—which today I must confess I lay far less importance upon—analyzing it into constituent parts, arguing it with my listeners without regard to the company I found myself in, devoting my whole time to the problem, which I found as wearisome as everybody else, but which —that was the difference—for that very reason I was resolved to pursue indefatigably until I solved it, so that I might be left free again to regard the ordinary, calm, happy life of every day. Just so have I, though with less childish means—yet the difference is not so very great—labored in the years since and go on laboring today.

But it began with that concert. I do not blame the concert; it is my innate disposition that has driven me on, and it would certainly have found some other opportunity of coming into action had the concert never taken place. Yet the fact that it happened so soon used to make me feel sorry for myself; it robbed me of a great part of my childhood; the blissful life of the young dog, which many can spin out for years, in my case lasted for only a few short months. So be it. There are more important things than childhood. And perhaps I have the prospect of far more childlike happiness, earned by a life of hard work, in my old age than any actual child would have the strength to bear, but which then I shall possess.

I began my inquiries with the simplest things; there was no lack of material; it is the actual superabundance, unfortunately, that casts me into despair in my darker hours. I began to inquire into the question what the canine race nourished itself upon. Now that is, if you like, by no means a simple question, of course; it has occupied us since the dawn of time, it is the chief object of all our meditation, countless observations and essays and views on this subject have been published, it has grown into a province of knowledge which in its prodigious compass is not only beyond the comprehension of any single scholar, but of all our scholars collectively, a burden which cannot be borne except by the whole of the dog community, and even then with difficulty and not quite in its totality; for it ever and again crumbles away like a neglected ancestral inheritance and must laboriously be rehabilitated anew—not to speak at all of the difficulties and almost unfulfillable conditions of my investigation. No one need point all this out to me, I know it all as well as any average dog; I have no ambition to meddle with real scientific matters, I have all the respect for knowledge that it deserves, but to increase knowledge I lack the equipment, the diligence, the leisure, and—not least, and particularly during the past few years—the desire as well. I swallow down my food, but the slightest preliminary methodical politico-economical observation of it does not seem to me worth while. In this connection the essence of all knowledge is enough for me, the simple rule with which the mother weans her young ones from her teats and sends them out into the world: "Water the ground as much as you can." And in this sentence is not almost everything contained? What has scientific inquiry, ever since our first fathers inaugurated it, of decisive importance to add to this? Mere details, mere details, and how uncertain they are: but this rule will remain as long as we are dogs. It concerns our main staple of food: true, we have also other resources, but only at a pinch, and if the year is not too bad we could live on this main staple of our food; this food we find on the earth, but the earth needs our water to nourish it and only at that price provides us with our food, the emergence of which, however, and this should not be forgotten, can also be hastened by certain spells, songs, and ritual movements. But in my opinion that is all; there is nothing else that is fundamental to be said on the question. In this opinion, moverover, I am at one with the vast majority of the dog community, and must firmly dissociate myself from all heretical views on this point. Quite honestly I have no ambition to be peculiar, or to pose as being in the right against the majority; I am only too happy when I can agree with my comrades, as I do in this case. My own inquiries, however, are in another direction. My personal observation tells me that the earth, when it is watered and scratched according to the rules of science, extrudes nourishment, and moreover in such quality, in such abundance, in such ways, in such places, at such hours as the laws partially or completely established by science demand. I accept all this; my question, however, is the following: "Whence does the earth procure this food?" A question which people in general pretend not to understand, and to which the best answer they can give is: "If you haven't enough to eat, we'll give you some of ours." Now consider this answer. I know that it is not one of the virtues of dogdom to share with others food that one has once gained possession of. Life is hard, the earth stubborn, science rich in knowledge but poor in practical results: anyone who has food keeps it to himself; that is not selfishness, but the opposite, dog law, the unanimous decision of the people, the outcome of their victory over egoism, for the possessors are always in a minority. And for that reason this answer: "If you haven't enough to eat, we'll give you some of ours" is merely a way of speaking, a jest, a form of raillery. I have not forgotten that. But all the more significant did it seem to me, when I was rushing about everywhere with my questions during those days, that they put mockery aside as far as I was concerned; true, they did not actually give me anything to eat—where could they have found it at a moment's notice?—and even if anyone chanced to have some food, naturally he forgot everything else in the fury of his hunger; yet they all seriously meant what they said when they made the offer, and here and there, right enough, I was presently allowed some slight trifle if I was only smart enough to snatch it quickly. How came it that people treated me so strangely, pampered me, favored me? Because I was a lean dog, badly fed and neglectful of my needs? But there were countless badly fed dogs running about, and the others snatched even the wretchedest scrap from under their noses whenever they could, and often not from greed, but rather on principle. No, they treated me with special favor; I cannot give much detailed proof of this, but I have a firm conviction that it was so. Was it my questions, then, that pleased them, and that they regarded as so clever? No, my questions did not please them and were generally looked on as stupid. And yet it could only have been my questions that won me their attention. It was as if they would rather do the impossible, that is, stop my mouth with food—they did not do it, but they would have liked to do it—than endure my questions. But in that case they would have done better to drive me away and refuse to listen to my questions. No, they did not want to do that; they did not indeed want to listen to my questions, but it was because I asked these questions that they did not want to drive me away. That was the time—much as I was ridiculed and treated as a silly puppy, and pushed here and pushed there—the time when I actually enjoyed most public esteem; never again was I to enjoy anything like it; I had free entry everywhere, no obstacle was put in my way, I was actually flattered, though the flattery was disguised as rudeness. And all really because of my questions, my impatience, my thirst for knowledge. Did they want to lull me to sleep, to divert me, without violence, almost lovingly, from a false path, yet a path whose falseness was not so completely beyond all doubt that violence was permissible? Also a certain respect and fear kept them from employing violence. I divined even in those days something of this; today I know it quite well, far better than those who actually practiced it at the time: what they wanted to do was really to divert me from my path. They did not succeed; they achieved the opposite; my vigilance was sharpened. More, it became clear to me that it was I who was trying to seduce the others, and that I was actually successful up to a certain point. Only with the assistance of the whole dog world could I begin to understand my own questions. For instance when I asked: "Whence does the earth procure this food?" was I troubled, as appearances might quite well indicate, about the earth; was I troubled about the labors of the earth? Not in the least; that, as I very soon recognized, was far from my mind; all that I cared for was the race of dogs, that and nothing else. For what is there actually except our own species? To whom but it can one appeal in the wide and empty world? All knowledge, the totality of all questions and all answers, is contained in the dog. If one could but realize this knowledge, if one could but bring it into the light of day, if we dogs would but own that we know infinitely more than we admit to ourselves! Even the most loquacious dog is more secretive of his knowledge than the places where good food can be found. Trembling with desire, whipping yourself with your own tail, you steal cautiously upon your fellow dog, you ask, you beg, you howl, you bite, and achieve —and achieve what you could have achieved just as well without any effort: amiable attention, friendly contiguity, honest acceptance, ardent embraces, barks that mingle as one: everything is directed towards achieving an ecstasy, a forgetting and finding again; but the one thing that you long to win above all, the admission of knowledge, remains denied to you. To such prayers, whether silent or loud, the only answers you get, even after you have employed your powers of seduction to the utmost, are vacant stares, averted glances, troubled and veiled eyes. It is much the same as it was when, a mere puppy, I shouted to the dog musicians and they remained silent.

Now one might say: "You complain about your fellow dogs, about their silence on crucial questions; you assert that they know more than they admit, more than they will allow to be valid, and that this silence, the mysterious reason for which is also, of course, tacitly concealed, poisons existence and makes it unendurable for you, so that you must either alter it or have done with it; that may be; but you are yourself a dog, you have also the dog knowledge; well, bring it out, not merely in the form of a question, but as an answer. If you utter it, who will think of opposing you? The great choir of dogdom will join in as if it had been waiting for you. Then you will have clarity, truth, avowal, as much of them as you desire. The roof of this wretched life, of which you say so many hard things, will burst open, and all of us, shoulder to shoulder, will ascend into the lofty realm of freedom. And if we should not achieve that final consummation, if things should become worse than before, if the whole truth should be more insupportable than the half-truth, if it should be proved that the silent are in the right as the guardians of existence, if the faint hope that we still possess should give way to complete hopelessness, the attempt is still worth the trial, since you do not desire to live as you are compelled to live. Well, then, why do you make it a reproach against the others that they are silent, and remain silent yourself?" Easy to answer: Because I am a dog; in essentials just as locked in silence as the others, stubbornly resisting my own questions, dour out of fear. To be precise, is it in the hope that they might answer me that I have questioned my fellow dogs, at least since my adult years? Have I any such foolish hope? Can I contemplate the foundations of our existence, divine their profundity, watch the labor of their construction, that dark labor, and expect all this to be forsaken, neglected, undone, simply because I ask a question? No, that I truly expect no longer. I understand my fellow dogs, am flesh of their flesh, of their miserable, ever-renewed, ever-desirous flesh. But it is not merely flesh and blood that we have in common, but knowledge also, and not only knowledge, but the key to it as well. I do not possess that key except in common with all the others; I cannot grasp it without their help. The hardest bones, containing the richest marrow, can be conquered only by a united crunching of all the teeth of all dogs. That of course is only a figure of speech and exaggerated; if all teeth were but ready they would not need even to bite, the bones would crack themselves and the marrow would be freely accessible to the feeblest of dogs. If I remain faithful to this metaphor, then the goal of my aims, my questions, my inquiries, appears monstrous, it is true. For I want to compel all dogs thus to assemble together, I want the bones to crack open under the pressure of their collective preparedness, and then I want to dismiss them to the ordinary life that they love, while all by myself, quite alone, I lap up the marrow. That sounds monstrous, almost as if I wanted to feed on the marrow, not merely of a bone, but of the whole canine race itself. But it is only a metaphor. The marrow that I am discussing here is no food; on the contrary, it is a poison.

My questions only serve as a goad to myself; I only want to be stimulated by the silence which rises up around me as the ultimate answer. "How long will you be able to endure the fact that the world of dogs, as your researches make more and more evident, is pledged to silence and always will be? How long will you be able to endure it?" That is the real great question of my life, before which all smaller ones sink into insignificance; it is put to myself alone and concerns no one else. Unfortunately I can answer it more easily than the smaller, specific questions: I shall probably hold out till my natural end; the calm of old age will put up a greater and greater resistance to all disturbing questions. I shall very likely die in silence and surrounded by silence, indeed almost peacefully, and I look forward to that with composure. An admirably strong heart, lungs that it is impossible to use up before their time, have been given to us dogs as if in malice; we survive all questions, even our own, bulwarks of silence that we are.

Recently I have taken more and more to casting up my life, looking for the decisive, the fundamental, error that I must surely have made; and I cannot find it. And yet I must have made it, for if I had not made it and yet were unable by the diligent labor of a long life to achieve my desire, that would prove that my desire is impossible, and complete hopelessness must follow. Behold, then, the work of a lifetime. First of all my inquiries into the question: Whence does the earth procure the food it gives us? A young dog, at bottom naturally greedy for life, I renounced all enjoyments, apprehensively avoided all pleasures, buried my head between my front paws when I was confronted by temptation, and addressed myself to my task. I was no scholar, neither in the information I acquired, nor in method, nor in intention. That was probably a defect, but it could not have been a decisive one. I had had little schooling, for I left my mother's care at an early age, soon got used to independence, led a free life; and premature independence is inimical to systematic learning. But I have seen much, listened to much, spoken with dogs of all sorts and conditions, understood everything, I believe, fairly intelligently, and correlated my particular observations fairly intelligently; that has compensated somewhat for my lack of scholarship, not to mention that independence, if it is a disadvantage in learning things, is an actual advantage when one is making one's own inquiries. In my case it was all the more necessary as I was not able to employ the real method of science, to avail myself, that is, of the labors of my predecessors, and establish contact with contemporary investigators. I was entirely cast on my own resources, began at the very beginning, and with the consciousness, inspiriting to youth, but utterly crushing to age, that the fortuitous point to which I carried my labors must also be the final one. Was I really so alone in my inquiries, at the beginning and up to now? Yes and no. It is inconceivable that there must not always have been and that there are not today individual dogs in the same case as myself. I cannot be so accursed as that. I do not deviate from the dog nature by a hairbreadth. Every dog has like me the impulse to question, and I have like every dog the impulse not to answer. Everyone has the impulse to question. How otherwise could my questions have affected my hearers in the slightest—and they were often affected, to my ecstatic delight, an exaggerated delight, I must confess—and how otherwise could I have been prevented from achieving much more than I have done? And that I have the compulsion to remain silent needs unfortunately no particular proof. I am at bottom, then, no different from any other dog; everybody, no matter how he may differ in opinion from me and reject my views, will gladly admit that, and I in turn will admit as much of any other dog. Only the mixture of the elements is different, a difference very important for the individual, insignificant for the race. And now can one credit that the composition of these available elements has never chanced through all the past and present to result in a mixture similar to mine, one, moreover, if mine be regarded as unfortunate, more unfortunate still? To think so would be contrary to all experience. We dogs are all engaged in the strangest occupations, occupations in which one would refuse to believe if one had not the most reliable information concerning them. The best example that I can quote is that of the soaring dog. The first time I heard of one I laughed and simply refused to believe it. What? One was asked to believe that there was a very tiny species of dog, not much bigger than my head even when it was full grown, and this dog, who must of course be a feeble creature, an artificial, weedy, brushed and curled fop by all accounts, incapable of making an honest jump, this dog was supposed, according to people's stories, to remain for the most part high up in the air, apparently doing nothing at all but simply resting there? No, to try to make me swallow such things was exploiting the simplicity of a young dog too outrageously, I told myself. But shortly afterwards I heard from another source an account of another soaring dog. Could there be a conspiracy to fool me? But after that I saw the dog musicians with my own eyes, and from that day I considered everything possible, no prejudices fettered my powers of apprehension, I investigated the most senseless rumors, following them as far as they could take me, and the most senseless seemed to me in this senseless world more probable than the sensible, and moreover particularly fertile for investigation. So it was too with the soaring dogs. I discovered a great many things about them; true, I have succeeded to this day in seeing none of them, but of their existence I have been firmly convinced for a long time, and they occupy an important place in my picture of the world. As usual, it is not, of course, their technique that chiefly gives me to think. It is wonderful—who can gainsay it?—that these dogs should be able to float in the air: in my amazed admiration for that I am at one with my fellow dogs. But far more strange to my mind is the senselessness, the dumb senselessness of these existences. They have no relation whatever to the general life of the community, they hover in the air, and that is all, and life goes on its usual way; someone now and then refers to art and artists, but there it ends. But why, my good dogs, why on earth do these dogs float in the air? What sense is there in their occupation? Why can one get no word of explanation regarding them? Why do they hover up there, letting their legs, the pride of dogs, fall into desuetude, preserving a detachment from the nourishing earth, reaping

without having sowed? being particularly well provided for,
as I hear, and at the cost of the dog community too. I can
flatter myself that my inquiries into these matters made some
stir. People began to investigate after a fashion, to collect
data; they made a beginning, at least, although they are never
likely to go farther. But after all that is something. And
though the truth will not be discovered by such means—
never can that stage be reached—yet they throw light on
some of the profounder ramifications of falsehood. For all the
senseless phenomena of our existence, and the most senseless most of all, are susceptible to investigation. Not completely, of course—that is the diabolical jest—but sufficiently
to spare one painful questions. Take the soaring dogs once
more as an example; they are not haughty as one might imagine at first, but rather particularly dependent upon their
fellow dogs; if one tries to put oneself in their place one
will see that. For they must do what they can to obtain
pardon, and not openly—that would be a violation of the
obligation to keep silence—they must do what they can to
obtain pardon for their way of life, or else divert attention
from it so that it may be forgotten—and they do this, I
have been told, by means of an almost unendurable volubility.
They are perpetually talking, partly of their philosophical
reflections, with which, seeing that they have completely renounced bodily exertion, they can continuously occupy themselves, partly of the observations which they have made from
their exalted stations; and although, as is very understandable
considering their lazy existence, they are not much distinguished for intellectual power, and their philosophy is as
worthless as their observations, and science can make hardly
any use of their utterances, and besides is not reduced to
draw assistance from such wretched sources, nevertheless if
one asks what the soaring dogs are really doing one will
invariably receive the reply that they contribute a great deal
to knowledge. "That is true," remarks someone, "but their

contributions are worthless and wearisome." The reply to
that is a shrug, or a change of the subject, or annoyance, or
laughter, and in a little while, when you ask again, you learn
once more that they contribute to knowledge, and finally
when you are asked the question you yourself will reply—
if you are not careful—to the same effect. And perhaps indeed
it is well not to be too obstinate, but to yield to public sentiment, to accept the extant soaring dogs, and without recogniz-
ing their right to existence, which cannot be done, yet to tolerate them. But more than this must not be required; that would
be going too far, and yet the demand is made. We are perpetually being asked to put up with new soaring dogs who are
always appearing. One does not even know where they come
from. Do these dogs multiply by propagation? Have they actually the strength for that?—for they are nothing much
more than a beautiful coat of hair, and what is there in that
to propagate? But even if that improbable contingency were
possible, when could it take place? For they are invariably
seen alone, self-complacently floating high up in the air, and
if once in a while they descend to take a run, it lasts only
for a minute or two, a few mincing struts and also always in
strict solitude, absorbed in what is supposed to be profound
thought, from which, even when they exert themselves to the
utmost, they cannot tear themselves free, or at least so they
say. But if they do not propagate their kind, is it credible
that there can be dogs who voluntarily give up life on the
solid ground, voluntarily become soaring dogs, and merely
for the sake of the comfort and a certain technical accom-
plishment choose that empty life on cushions up there? It
is unthinkable; neither propagation nor voluntary transition
is thinkable. The facts, however, show that there are always
new soaring dogs in evidence; from which one must conclude
that, in spite of obstacles which appear insurmountable to our
understanding, no dog species, however curious, ever dies
out, once it exists, or, at least, not without a tough struggle,

not without being capable of putting up a successful defense for a long time.

But if that is valid for such an out-of-the-way, externally odd, inefficient species as the soaring dog, must I not also accept it as valid for mine? Besides, I am not in the least queer outwardly; an ordinary middle-class dog such as is very prevalent, in this neighborhood, at least, I am neither particularly exceptional in any way, nor particularly repellent in any way; and in my youth and to some extent also in maturity, so long as I attended to my appearance and had lots of exercise, I was actually considered a very handsome dog. My front view was particularly admired, my slim legs, the fine set of my head; but my silvery white and yellow coat, which curled only at the hair tips, was very pleasing too; in all that there was nothing strange; the only strange thing about me is my nature, yet even that, as I am always careful to remember, has its foundation in universal dog nature. Now if not even the soaring dogs live in isolation, but invariably manage to encounter their fellows somewhere or other in the great dog world, and even to conjure new generations of themselves out of nothingness, then I too can live in the confidence that I am not quite forlorn. Certainly the fate of types like mine must be a strange one, and the existence of my colleagues can never be of visible help to me, if for no other reason than that I should scarcely ever be able to recognize them. We are the dogs who are crushed by the silence, who long to break through it, literally to get a breath of fresh air; the others seem to thrive on silence: true, that is only so in appearance, as in the case of the musical dogs, who ostensibly were quite calm when they played, but in reality were in a state of intense excitement; nevertheless the illusion is very strong, one tries to make a breach in it, but it mocks every attempt. What help, then, do my colleagues find? What kind of attempts do they make to manage to go on living in spite of everything? These attempts may be of various kinds. My own bout of questioning while I was young was one. So I thought that perhaps if I associated with those who asked many questions I might find my real comrades. Well, I did so for some time, with great self-control, a self-control made necessary by the annoyance I felt when I was interrupted by perpetual questions that I mostly could not answer myself: for the only thing that concerns me is to obtain answers. Moreover, who but is eager to ask questions when he is young, and how, when so many questions are going about, are you to pick out the right questions? One question sounds like another; it is the intention that counts, but that is often hidden even from the questioner. And besides, it is a peculiarity of dogs to be always asking questions, they ask them confusedly all together; it is as if in doing that they were trying to obliterate every trace of the genuine questions. No, my real colleagues are not to be found among the youthful questioners, and just as little among the old and silent, to whom I now belong. But what good are all these questions, for they have failed me completely; apparently my colleagues are cleverer dogs than I, and have recourse to other excellent methods that enable them to bear this life, methods which, nevertheless, as I can tell from my own experience, though they may perhaps help at a pinch, though they may calm, lull to rest, distract, are yet on the whole as impotent as my own, for, no matter where I look, I can see no sign of their success. I am afraid that the last thing by which I can hope to recognize my real colleagues is their success. But where, then, are my real colleagues? Yes, that is the burden of my complaint; that is the kernel of it. Where are they? Everywhere and nowhere. Perhaps my next-door neighbor, only three jumps away, is one of them; we often bark across to each other, he calls on me sometimes too, though I do not call on him. Is he my real colleague? I do not know, I certainly see no sign of it in him, but it is possible. It is possible, but all the same nothing is more improbable. When he is away I can amuse myself, drawing on my fancy, by discovering in him many things that have a suspicious resemblance to myself; but once he stands before me all my fancies become ridiculous. An old dog, a little smaller even than myself—and I am hardly medium size —brown, short-haired, with a tired hang of the head and a shuffling gait; on top of all this he trails his left hind leg behind him a little because of some disease. For a long time now I have been more intimate with him than with anybody else; I am glad to say that I can still get on tolerably well with him, and when he goes away I shout the most friendly greetings after him, though not out of affection, but in anger at myself; for if I follow him I find him just as disgusting again, slinking along there with his trailing leg and his much too low hindquarters. Sometimes it seems to me as if I were trying to humiliate myself by thinking of him as my colleague. Nor in our talks does he betray any trace of similarity of thought; true, he is clever and cultured enough as these things go here, and I could learn much from him; but is it for cleverness and culture that I am looking? We converse usually about local questions, and I am astonished —my isolation has made me more clear-sighted in such matters—how much intelligence is needed even by an ordinary dog, even in average and not unfavorable circumstances, if he is to live out his life and defend himself against the greater of life's customary dangers. True, knowledge provides the rules one must follow, but even to grasp them imperfectly and in rough outline is by no means easy, and when one has actually grasped them the real difficulty still remains, namely to apply them to local conditions—here almost nobody can help, almost every hour brings new tasks, and every new patch of earth its specific problems; no one can maintain that he has settled everything for good and that henceforth his life will go on, so to speak, of itself, not even I myself, though my needs shrink literally from day to day. And all this ceaseless labor—to what end? Merely to entomb oneself deeper and deeper in silence, it seems, so deep that one can never be dragged out of it again by anybody.

People often praise the universal progress made by the dog community throughout the ages, and probably mean by that more particularly the progress in knowledge. Certainly knowledge is progressing, its advance is irresistible, it actually progresses at an accelerating speed, always faster, but what is there to praise in that? It is as if one were to praise someone because with the years he grows older, and in consequence comes nearer and nearer to death with increasing speed. That is a natural and moreover an ugly process, in which I find nothing to praise. I can only see decline everywhere, in saying which, however, I do not mean that earlier generations were essentially better than ours, but only younger; that was their great advantage, their memory was not so overburdened as ours today, it was easier to get them to speak out, and even if nobody actually succeeded in doing that, the possibility of it was greater, and it is indeed this greater sense of possibility that moves us so deeply when we listen to those old and strangely simple stories. Here and there we catch a curiously significant phrase and we would almost like to leap to our feet, if we did not feel the weight of centuries upon us. No, whatever objection I may have to my age, former generations were not better, indeed in a sense they were far worse, far weaker. Even in those days wonders did not openly walk the streets for anyone to seize; but all the same, dogs— I cannot put it in any other way—had not yet become so doggish as today, the edifice of dogdom was still loosely put together, the true Word could still have intervened, planning or replanning the structure, changing it at will, transforming it into its opposite; and the Word was there, was very near at least, on the tip of everybody's tongue, anyone might have hit upon it. And what has become of it today? Today one may pluck out one's very heart and not find it. Our generation is lost, it may be, but it is more blameless than those earlier ones. I can understand the hesitation of my generation, indeed it is no longer mere hesitation; it is the thousandth forgetting of a dream dreamt a thousand times and forgotten a thousand times; and who can damn us merely for forgetting for the thousandth time? But I fancy I understand the hesitation of our forefathers too, we would probably have acted just as they did; indeed I could almost say: well for us that it was not we who had to take the guilt upon us, that instead we can hasten in almost guiltless silence towards death in a world darkened by others. When our first fathers strayed they had doubtless scarcely any notion that their aberration was to be an endless one, they could still literally see the crossroads, it seemed an easy matter to turn back whenever they pleased, and if they hesitated to turn back it was merely because they wanted to enjoy a dog's life for a little while longer; it was not yet a genuine dog's life, and already it seemed intoxicatingly beautiful to them, so what must it become in a little while, a very little while, and so they strayed farther. They did not know what we can now guess at, contemplating the course of history: that change begins in the soul before it appears in ordinary existence, and that, when they began to enjoy a dog's life, they must already have possessed real old dogs' souls, and were by no means so near their starting point as they thought, or as their eyes feasting on all doggish joys tried to persuade them. But who can still speak of youth today? These were the really young dogs, but their sole ambition unfortunately was to become old dogs, truly a thing which they could not fail to achieve, as all succeeding generations show, and ours, the last, most clearly of all.

Naturally I do not talk to my neighbor of these things, but often I cannot but think of them when I am sitting opposite him—that typical old dog—or bury my nose in his coat, which already has a whiff of the smell of cast-off hides.

To talk to him, or even to any of the others, about such
things would be pointless. I know what course the conversation would take. He would urge a slight objection now and
then, but finally he would agree—agreement is the best
weapon of defense—and the matter would be buried: why
indeed trouble to exhume it at all? And in spite of this there
is a profounder understanding between my neighbor and me,
going deeper than mere words. I shall never cease to maintain that, though I have no proof of it and perhaps am
merely suffering from an ordinary delusion, caused by the
fact that for a long time this dog has been the only one with
whom I have held any communication, and so I am bound
to cling to him. "Are you after all my colleague in your own
fashion? And ashamed because everything has miscarried with
you? Look, the same fate has been mine. When I am alone
I weep over it; come, it is sweeter to weep in company." I
often have such thoughts as these and then I give him a
prolonged look. He does not lower his glance, but neither can
one read anything from it; he gazes at me dully, wondering
why I am silent and why I have broken off the conversation.
But perhaps that very glance is his way of questioning me,
and I disappoint him just as he disappoints me. In my youth,
if other problems had not been more important to me then,
and I had not been perfectly satisfied with my own company,
I would probably have asked him straight out and received
an answer flatly agreeing with me, and that would have been
worse even than today's silence. But is not everybody silent
exactly in the same way? What is there to prevent me from
believing that everyone is my colleague, instead of thinking
that I have only one or two fellow inquirers—lost and forgotten along with their petty achievements, so that I can
never reach them by any road through the darkness of ages or
the confused throng of the present: why not believe that all
dogs from the beginning of time have been my colleagues,
all diligent in their own way, all unsuccessful in their own

way, all silent or falsely garrulous in their own way, as hopeless research is apt to make one? But in that case I need not have severed myself from my fellows at all, I could have remained quietly among the others, I had no need to fight my way out like a stubborn child through the closed ranks of the grown-ups, who indeed wanted as much as I to find a way out, and who seemed incomprehensible to me simply because of their knowledge, which told them that nobody could ever escape and that it was stupid to use force.

Such ideas, however, are definitely due to the influence of my neighbor; he confuses me, he fills me with dejection; and yet in himself he is happy enough, at least when he is in his own quarters I often hear him shouting and singing; it is really unbearable. It would be a good thing to renounce this last tie also, to cease giving way to the vague dreams which all contact with dogs unavoidably provokes, no matter how hardened one may consider oneself, and to employ the short time that still remains for me exclusively in prosecuting my researches. The next time he comes I shall slip away, or pretend I am asleep, and keep up the pretense until he stops visiting me.

Also my researches have fallen into desuetude, I relax, I grow weary, I trot mechanically where once I raced enthusiastically. I think of the time when I began to inquire into the question: "Whence does the earth procure this food?" Then indeed I really lived among the people, I pushed my way where the crowd was thickest, wanted everybody to know my work and be my audience, and my audience was even more essential to me than my work; I still expected to produce some effect or other, and that naturally gave me a great impetus, which now that I am solitary is gone. But in those days I was so full of strength that I achieved something unprecedented, something at variance with all our principles, and that every contemporary eyewitness assuredly recalls now as an uncanny feat. Our scientific knowledge, which generally

makes for an extreme specialization, is remarkably simple in
one province. I mean where it teaches that the earth en-
genders our food, and then, after having laid down this hypothesis, gives the methods by which the different foods
may be achieved in their best kinds and greatest abundance.
Now it is of course true that the earth brings forth all food,
of that there can be no doubt; but as simple as people
generally imagine it to be the matter is not; and their belief that it is simple prevents further inquiry. Take an ordinary occurrence that happens every day. If we were to
be quite inactive, as I am almost completely now, and
after a perfunctory scratching and watering of the soil lay
down and waited for what was to come, then we should find
the food on the ground, assuming, that is, that a result of
some kind is inevitable. Nevertheless that is not what usually
happens. Those who have preserved even a little freedom of
judgment on scientific matters—and their numbers are truly
small, for science draws a wider and wider circle around itself
—will easily see, without having to make any specific experiment, that the main part of the food that is discovered on the
ground in such cases comes from above; indeed customarily
we snap up most of our food, according to our dexterity and
greed, before it has reached the ground at all. In saying that,
however, I am saying nothing against science; the earth, of
course, brings forth this kind of food too. Whether the earth
draws one kind of food out of itself and calls down another
kind from the skies perhaps makes no essential difference, and
science, which has established that in both cases it is necessary to prepare the ground, need not perhaps concern itself
with such distinctions, for does it not say: "If you have food
in your jaws you have solved all questions for the time being."
But it seems to me that science nevertheless takes a veiled interest, at least to some extent, in these matters, inasmuch
as it recognizes two chief methods of procuring food; namely
the actual preparation of the ground, and secondly the auxili-

ary perfecting processes of incantation, dance, and song. I find here a distinction in accordance with the one I have myself made; not a definitive distinction, perhaps, but yet clear enough. The scratching and watering of the ground, in my opinion, serves to produce both kinds of food, and remains indispensable; incantation, dance, and song, however, are concerned less with the ground food in the narrower sense, and serve principally to attract the food from above. Tradition fortifies me in this interpretation. The ordinary dogs themselves set science right here without knowing it, and without science being able to venture a word in reply. If, as science claims, these ceremonies minister only to the soil, giving it the potency, let us say, to attract food from the air, then logically they should be directed exclusively to the soil; it is the soil that the incantations must be whispered to, the soil that must be danced to. And to the best of my knowledge science ordains nothing else than this. But now comes the remarkable thing; the people in all their ceremonies gaze upwards. This is no insult to science, since science does not forbid it, but leaves the husbandman complete freedom in this respect; in its teaching it takes only the soil into account, and if the husbandman carries out its instructions concerning the preparation of the ground it is content; yet, in my opinion, it should really demand more than this if it is logical. And, though I have never been deeply initiated into science, I simply cannot conceive how the learned can bear to let our people, unruly and passionate as they are, chant their incantations with their faces turned upwards, wail our ancient folk songs into the air, and spring high in their dances as though, forgetting the ground, they wished to take flight from it for ever. I took this contradiction as my starting point, and whenever, according to the teachings of science, the harvest time was approaching, I restricted my attention to the ground, it was the ground that I scratched in the dance, and I almost gave myself a crick in the neck keeping my head as close to the ground as I could. Later I dug a hole for my nose, and sang and declaimed into it so that only the ground might hear, and nobody else beside or above me.

The results of my experiment were meager. Sometimes the food did not appear, and I was already preparing to rejoice at this proof, but then the food would appear; it was exactly as if my strange performance had caused some confusion at first, but had shown itself later to possess advantages, so that in my case the usual barking and leaping could be dispensed with. Often, indeed, the food appeared in greater abundance than formerly, but then again it would stay away altogether. With a diligence hitherto unknown in a young dog I drew up exact reports of all my experiments, fancied that here and there I was on a scent that might lead me further, but then it lost itself again in obscurity. My inadequate grounding in science also undoubtedly held me up here. What guarantee had I, for instance, that the absence of the food was not caused by unscientific preparation of the ground rather than by my experiments, and if that should be so, then all my conclusions were invalid. In certain circumstances I might have been able to achieve an almost scrupulously exact experiment; namely, if I had succeeded only once in bringing down food by an upward incantation without preparing the ground at all, and then had failed to extract food by an incantation directed exclusively to the ground. I attempted indeed something of this kind, but without any real belief in it and without the conditions being quite perfect; for it is my fixed opinion that a certain amount of ground-preparation is always necessary, and even if the heretics who deny this are right, their theory can never be proved in any case, seeing that the watering of the ground is done under a kind of compulsion, and within certain limits simply cannot be avoided. Another and somewhat tangential experiment succeeded better and aroused some public attention. Arguing from the customary method of snatching food while still in the air, I decided to allow the food to fall to the ground, but to make no effort to snatch it. Accordingly I always made a small jump in the air when the food appeared, but timed it so that it might always fail of its object; in the majority of instances the food fell dully and indifferently to the ground in spite of this, and I flung myself furiously upon it, with the fury both of hunger and of disappointment. But in isolated cases something else happened, something really strange; the food did not fall but followed me through the air; the food pursued the hungry. That never went on for long, always for only a short stretch, then the food fell after all, or vanished completely, or—the most common case—my greed put a premature end to the experiment and I swallowed down the tempting food. All the same I was happy at that time, a stir of curiosity ran through my neighborhood, I attracted uneasy attention, I found my acquaintances more accessible to my questions, I could see in their eyes a gleam that seemed like an appeal for help; and even if it was only the reflection of my own glance I asked for nothing more. I was satisfied. Until at last I discovered—and the others discovered it simultaneously—that this experiment of mine was a commonplace of science, had already succeeded with others far more brilliantly than with me, and though it had not been attempted for a long time on account of the extreme self-control it required, had also no need to be repeated, for scientifically it had no value at all. It only proved what was already known, that the ground not only attracts food vertically from above, but also at a slant, indeed sometimes in spirals. So there I was left with my experiment, but I was not discouraged, I was too young for that; on the contrary, this disappointment braced me to attempt perhaps the greatest achievement of my life. I did not believe the scientists' depreciations of my experiment, yet belief was of no avail here, but only proof, and I resolved to set about establishing that and thus raise my experiment from its original irrelevance and set it in the very center of the field of research. I wished to prove that when I retreated before the food it was not the ground that attracted it at a slant, but I who drew it after me. This first experiment, it is true, I could not carry any farther; to see the food before one and experiment in a scientific spirit at the same time—one cannot keep that up indefinitely. But I decided to do something else; I resolved to fast completely as long as I could stand it, and at the same time avoid all sight of food, all temptation. If I were to withdraw myself in this manner, remain lying day and night with closed eyes, trouble myself neither to snatch food from the air nor to lift it from the ground, and if, as I dared not expect, yet faintly hoped, without taking any of the customary measures, and merely in response to the unavoidable irrational watering of the ground and the quiet recitation of the incantations and songs (the dance I wished to omit, so as not to weaken my powers) the food were to come of itself from above, and without going near the ground were to knock at my teeth for admittance—if that were to happen, then, even if science was not confuted, for it has enough elasticity to admit exceptions and isolated cases—I asked myself what would the other dogs say, who fortunately do not possess such extreme elasticity? For this would be no exceptional case like those handed down by history, such as the incident, let us say, of the dog who refuses, because of bodily illness or trouble of mind, to prepare the ground, to track down and seize his food, upon which the whole dog community recite magical formulae and by this means succeed in making the food deviate from its customary route into the jaws of the invalid. I, on the contrary, was perfectly sound and at the height of my powers, my appetite so splendid that it prevented me all day from thinking of anything but itself; I submitted, moreover, whether it be credited or not, voluntarily to my period of fasting, was myself quite able to conjure down my

own supply of food and wished also to do so, and so I asked
no assistance from the dog community, and indeed rejected
it in the most determined manner.

I sought a suitable place for myself in an outlying clump
of bushes, where I would have to listen to no talk of food,
no sound of munching jaws and bones being gnawed; I ate
my fill for the last time and laid me down. As far as possible
I wanted to pass my whole time with closed eyes; until the
food came it would be perpetual night for me, even though
my vigil might last for days or weeks. During that time, however, I dared not sleep much, better indeed if I did not
sleep at all—and that made everything much harder—for I
must not only conjure the food down from the air, but also
be on my guard lest I should be asleep when it arrived; yet
on the other hand sleep would be very welcome to me, for
I would manage to fast much longer asleep than awake. For
those reasons I decided to arrange my time prudently and
sleep a great deal, but always in short snatches. I achieved
this by always resting my head while I slept on some frail
twig, which soon snapped and so awoke me. So there I lay,
sleeping or keeping watch, dreaming or singing quietly to
myself. My first vigils passed uneventfully; perhaps in the
place whence the food came no one had yet noticed that I
was lying there in resistance to the normal course of things,
and so there was no sign. I was a little disturbed in my con-
centration by the fear that the other dogs might miss me,
presently find me, and attempt something or other against
me. A second fear was that at the mere wetting of the
ground, though it was unfruitful ground according to the
findings of science, some chance nourishment might appear
and seduce me by its smell. But for a time nothing of that
kind happened and I could go on fasting. Apart from such
fears I was more calm during this first stage than I could remember ever having been before. Although in reality I was
laboring to annul the findings of science, I felt within me

a deep reassurance, indeed almost the proverbial serenity of
the scientific worker. In my thoughts I begged forgiveness of
science; there must be room in it for my researches too; con-
solingly in my ears rang the assurance that no matter how
great the effect of my inquiries might be, and indeed the
greater the better, I would not be lost to ordinary dog life;
science regarded my attempts with benevolence, it itself would
undertake the interpretation of my discoveries, and that prom-
ise already meant fulfillment; while until now I had felt out-
lawed in my innermost heart and had run my head against
the traditional walls of my species like a savage, I would now
be accepted with great honor, the long-yearned-for warmth
of assembled canine bodies would lap around me, I would
ride uplifted high on the shoulders of my fellows. Remarkable
effects of my first hunger. My achievement seemed so great
to me that I began to weep with emotion and self-pity there
among the quiet bushes, which it must be confessed was not
very understandable, for when I was looking forward to my
well-earned reward why should I weep? Probably out of pure
happiness. It is always when I am happy, and that is seldom
enough, that I weep. After that, however, these feelings soon
passed. My beautiful fancies fled one by one before the
increasing urgency of my hunger; a little longer and I was,
after an abrupt farewell to all my imaginations and my
sublime feelings, totally alone with the hunger burning in
my entrails. "That is my hunger," I told myself countless
times during this stage, as if I wanted to convince myself that
my hunger and I were still two things and I could shake it
off like a burdensome lover; but in reality we were very painfully one, and when I explained to myself: "That is my
hunger," it was really my hunger that was speaking and having
its joke at my expense. A bad, bad time! I still shudder to
think of it, and not merely on account of the suffering I
endured then, but mainly because I was unable to finish it
then and consequently shall have to live through that suffering

once more if I am ever to achieve anything; for today I still hold fasting to be the final and most potent means of my research. The way goes through fasting; the highest, if it is attainable, is attainable only by the highest effort, and the highest effort among us is voluntary fasting. So when I think of those times—and I would gladly pass my life in brooding over them—I cannot help thinking also of the time that still threatens me. It seems to me that it takes almost a lifetime to recuperate from such an attempt; my whole life as an adult lies between me and that fast, and I have not recovered yet. When I begin upon my next fast I shall perhaps have more resolution than the first time, because of my greater experience and deeper insight into the need for the attempt, but my powers are still enfeebled by that first essay, and so I shall probably begin to fail at the mere approach of these familiar horrors. My weaker appetite will not help me; it will only reduce the value of the attempt a little, and will, indeed, probably force me to fast longer than would have been necessary the first time. I think I am clear on these and many other matters, the long interval has not been wanting in trial attempts, often enough I have literally got my teeth into hunger; but I was still not strong enough for the ultimate effort, and now the unspoilt ardor of youth is of course gone for ever. It vanished in the great privations of that first fast. All sorts of thoughts tormented me. Our forefathers appeared threateningly before me. True, I held them responsible for everything, even if I dared not say so openly; it was they who involved our dog life in guilt, and so I could easily have responded to their menaces with countermenaces; but I bow before their knowledge, it came from sources of which we know no longer, and for that reason, much as I may feel compelled to oppose them, I shall never actually overstep their laws, but content myself with wriggling out through the gaps, for which I have a particularly good nose. On the question of fasting I appealed to the well-known dialogue in the course of which one

of our sages once expressed the intention of forbidding fasting, but was dissuaded by a second with the words: "But who
would ever think of fasting?" whereupon the first sage allowed
himself to be persuaded and withdrew the prohibition. But
now arises the question: "Is not fasting really forbidden after
all?" The great majority of commentators deny this and regard
fasting as freely permitted, and holding as they think with the
second sage do not worry in the least about the evil consequences that may result from erroneous interpretations. I had
naturally assured myself on this point before I began my
fast. But now that I was twisted with the pangs of hunger,
and in my distress of mind sought relief in my own hind legs,
despairingly licking and gnawing at them up to the very but-
tocks, the universal interpretation of this dialogue seemed to
me entirely and completely false, I cursed the commentators'
science, I cursed myself for having been led astray by it; for
the dialogue contained, as any child could see, more than
merely one prohibition of fasting; the first sage wished to
forbid fasting; what a sage wishes is already done, so fasting
was forbidden; as for the second sage, he not only agreed with
the first, but actually considered fasting impossible, piled therefore on the first prohibition a second, that of dog nature itself;
the first sage saw this and thereupon withdrew the explicit
prohibition, that was to say, he imposed upon all dogs, the
matter being now settled, the obligation to know themselves
and to make their own prohibitions regarding fasting. So here
was a threefold prohibition instead of merely one, and I had
violated it. Now I could at least have obeyed at this point,
though tardily, but in the midst of my pain I felt a longing
to go on fasting, and I followed it as greedily as if it were a
strange dog. I could not stop; perhaps too I was already too
weak to get up and seek safety for myself in familiar scenes.
I tossed about on the fallen forest leaves, I could no longer
sleep, I heard noises on every side; the world, which had been
asleep during my life hitherto, seemed to have been awakened

by my fasting, I was tortured by the fancy that I would never
be able to eat again, and I must eat so as to reduce to silence
this world rioting so noisily around me, and I would never
be able to do so; but the greatest noise of all came from my
own belly, I often laid my ear against it with startled eyes,
for I could hardly believe what I heard. And now that things
were becoming unendurable my very nature seemed to be
seized by the general frenzy, and made senseless attempts to
save itself; the smell of food began to assail me, delicious dain-
ties that I had long since forgotten, delights of my childhood;
yes, I could smell the very fragrance of my mother's teats; I
forgot my resolution to resist all smells, or rather I did not
forget it; I dragged myself to and fro, never for more than a
few yards, and sniffed as if that were in accordance with my
resolution, as if I were looking for food simply to be on my
guard against it. The fact that I found nothing did not disappoint me; the food must be there, only it was always a
few steps away, my legs failed me before I could reach it.
But simultaneously I knew that nothing was there, and that
I made those feeble movements simply out of fear lest I might
collapse in this place and never be able to leave it. My last
hopes, my last dreams vanished; I would perish here miserably;
of what use were my researches?—childish attempts undertaken in childish and far happier days; here and now was the
hour of deadly earnest, here my inquiries should have shown
their value, but where had they vanished? Only a dog lay here
helplessly snapping at the empty air, a dog who, though he
still watered the ground with convulsive haste at short intervals and without being aware of it, could not remember even
the shortest of the countless incantations stored in his memory,
not even the little rhyme which the newly born puppy says
when it snuggles under its mother. It seemed to me as if I
were separated from all my fellows, not by a quite short stretch,
but by an infinite distance, and as if I would die less of hunger
than of neglect. For it was clear that nobody troubled about

me, nobody beneath the earth, on it, or above it; I was dying of their indifference; they said indifferently: "He is dying," and it would actually come to pass. And did I not myself assent? Did I not say the same thing? Had I not wanted to be forsaken like this? Yes, brothers, but not so as to perish in that place, but to achieve truth and escape from this world of falsehood, where there is no one from whom you can learn the truth, not even from me, born as I am a citizen of falsehood. Perhaps the truth was not so very far off, and I not so forsaken, therefore, as I thought; or I may have been forsaken less by my fellows than by myself, in yielding and consenting to die.

But one does not die so easily as a nervous dog imagines. I merely fainted, and when I came to and raised my eyes a strange hound was standing before me. I did not feel hungry, but rather filled with strength, and my limbs, it seemed to me, were light and agile, though I made no attempt to prove this by getting to my feet. My visual faculties in themselves were no keener than usual; a beautiful but not at all extraordinary hound stood before me; I could see that, and that was all, and yet it seemed to me that I saw something more in him. There was blood under me, at first I took it for food; but I recognized it immediately as blood that I had vomited. I turned my eyes from it to the strange hound. He was lean, long-legged, brown with a patch of white here and there, and had a fine, strong, piercing glance. "What are you doing here?" he asked. "You must leave this place." "I can't leave it just now," I said, without trying to explain, for how could I explain everything to him; besides, he seemed to be in a hurry. "Please go away," he said, impatiently lifting his feet and setting them down again. "Let me be," I said, "leave me to myself and don't worry about me; the others don't." "I ask you to go for your own sake," he said. "You can ask for any reason you like," I replied. "I can't go even if I wanted to." "You need have no fear of that," he said, smiling. "You can go all right. It's because you seem to be feeble that I ask you to go now, and you can go slowly if you like; if you linger now you'll have to race off later on." "That's my affair," I replied. "It's mine too," he said, saddened by my stubbornness, yet obviously resolved to let me lie for the time being, but at the same time to seize the opportunity of paying court to me. At any other time I would gladly have submitted to the blandishments of such a beautiful creature, but at that moment, why, I cannot tell, the thought filled me with terror. "Get out!" I screamed, and all the louder as I had no other means of protecting my-self. "All right, I'll leave you then," he said, slowly retreating. "You're wonderful. Don't I please you?" "You'll please me by going away and leaving me in peace," I said, but I was no longer so sure of myself as I tried to make him think. My senses, sharpened by fasting, suddenly seemed to see or hear something about him; it was just beginning, it was growing, it came nearer, and I knew that this hound had the power to drive me away, even if I could not imagine to myself at the moment how I was ever to get to my feet. And I gazed at him—he had merely shaken his head sadly at my rough answer—with ever-mounting desire. "Who are you?" I asked. "I'm a hunter," he replied. "And why won't you let me lie here?" I asked. "You disturb me," he said. "I can't hunt while you're here." "Try," I said, "perhaps you'll be able to hunt after all." "No," he said, "I'm sorry, but you must go." "Don't hunt for this one day!" I implored him. "No," he said, "I must hunt." "I must go; you must hunt," I said, "nothing but musts. Can you explain to me why we must?" "No," he replied, "but there's nothing that needs to be explained, these are natural, self-evident things." "Not quite so self-evident as all that," I said, "you're sorry that you must drive me away, and yet you do it." "That's so," he replied. "That's so," I echoed him crossly, "that isn't an answer. Which sacrifice would you rather make: to give up your hunting, or give up driving me away?" "To give up my hunting," he said without

hesitation. "There!" said I, "don't you see that you're contradicting yourself?" "How am I contradicting myself?" he
replied. "My dear little dog, can it be that you really don't
understand that I must? Don't you understand the most self-
evident fact?" I made no answer, for I noticed—and new life
ran through me, life such as terror gives—I noticed from
almost invisible indications, which perhaps nobody but myself
could have noticed, that in the depths of his chest the hound
was preparing to upraise a song. "You're going to sing," I
said. "Yes," he replied gravely, "I'm going to sing, soon, but
not yet." "You're beginning already," I said. "No," he said,
"not yet. But be prepared." "I can hear it already, though
you deny it," I said, trembling. He was silent, and then I
thought I saw something such as no dog before me had ever
seen, at least there is no slightest hint of it in our tradition,
and I hastily bowed my head in infinite fear and shame in the
pool of blood lying before me. I thought I saw that the hound
was already singing without knowing it, nay, more, that the
melody, separated from him, was floating on the air in accordance with its own laws, and, as though he had no part in
it, was moving towards me, towards me alone. Today, of
course, I deny the validity of all such perceptions and ascribe
them to my over-excitation at that time, but even if it was an
error it had nevertheless a sort of grandeur, and is the sole,
even if delusive, reality that I have carried over into this world
from my period of fasting, and shows at least how far we
can go when we are beyond ourselves. And I was actually quite
beyond myself. In ordinary circumstances I would have been
very ill, incapable of moving; but the melody, which the
hound soon seemed to acknowledge as his, was quite irresistible. It grew stronger and stronger; its waxing power seemed
to have no limits, and already almost burst my eardrums. But
the worst was that it seemed to exist solely for my sake, this
voice before whose sublimity the woods fell silent, to exist
solely for my sake; who was I, that I could dare to remain here,

lying brazenly before it in my pool of blood and filth. I tottered to my feet and looked down at myself; this wretched body can never run, I still had time to think, but already, spurred on by the melody, I was careering from the spot in splendid style. I said nothing to my friends; probably I could have told them all when I first arrived, but I was too feeble, and later it seemed to me that such things could not be told. Hints which I could not refrain from occasionally dropping were quite lost in the general conversation. For the rest I recovered physically in a few hours, but spiritually I still suffer from the effects of that experiment.

Nevertheless, I next carried my researches into music. True, science had not been idle in this sphere either; the science of music, if I am correctly informed, is perhaps still more comprehensive than that of nurture, and in any case established on a firmer basis. That may be explained by the fact that this province admits of more objective inquiry than the other, and its knowledge is more a matter of pure observation and systematization, while in the province of food the main object is to achieve practical results. That is the reason why the science of music is accorded greater esteem than that of nurture, but also why the former has never penetrated so deeply into the life of the people. I myself felt less attracted to the science of music than to any other until I heard that voice in the forest. My experience with the musical dogs had indeed drawn my attention to music, but I was still too young at that time. Nor is it by any means easy even to come to grips with that science; it is regarded as very esoteric and politely excludes the crowd. Besides, although what struck me most deeply at first about these dogs was their music, their silence seemed to me still more significant; as for their affrighting music, probably it was quite unique, so that I could leave it out of account; but thenceforth their silence confronted me everywhere and in all the dogs I met. So for penetrating into real dog nature research into food seemed to me the best method, calculated to lead me to my goal by the straightest path. Perhaps I was mistaken. A border region between these two sciences, however, had already attracted my attention. I mean the theory of incantation, by which food is called down. Here again it is very much against me that I have never seriously tackled the science of music and in this sphere cannot even count myself among the half-educated, the class on whom science looks down most of all. This fact I cannot get away from. I could not—I have proof of that, unfortunately —I could not pass even the most elementary scientific examination set by an authority on the subject. Of course, quite apart from the circumstances already mentioned, the reason for that can be found in my incapacity for scientific investigation, my limited powers of thought, my bad memory, but above all in my inability to keep my scientific aim continuously before my eyes. All this I frankly admit, even with a certain degree of pleasure. For the more profound cause of my scientific incapacity seems to me to be an instinct, and indeed by no means a bad one. If I wanted to brag I might say that it was this very instinct that invalidated my scientific capacities, for it would surely be a very extraordinary thing if one who shows a tolerable degree of intelligence in dealing with the ordinary daily business of life, which certainly cannot be called simple, and moreover one whose findings have been checked and verified, where that was possible, by individual scientists if not by science itself, should *a priori* be incapable of planting his paw even on the first rung of the ladder of science. It was this instinct that made me—and perhaps for the sake of science itself, but a different science from that of today, an ultimate science—prize freedom higher than everything else. Freedom! Certainly such freedom as is possible today is a wretched business. But nevertheless freedom, nevertheless a possession.

THE BURROW

I HAVE completed the construction of my burrow and it seems to be successful. All that can be seen from outside is a big hole; that, however, really leads nowhere; if you take a few steps you strike against natural firm rock. I can make no boast of having contrived this ruse intentionally; it is simply the remains of one of my many abortive building attempts, but finally it seemed to me advisable to leave this one hole without filling it in. True, some ruses are so subtle that they defeat themselves, I know that better than anyone, and it is certainly a risk to draw attention by this hole to the fact that there may be something in the vicinity worth inquiring into. But you do not know me if you think I am afraid, or that I built my burrow simply out of fear. At a distance of some thousand paces from this hole lies, covered by a movable layer of moss, the real entrance to the burrow; it is secured as safely as anything in this world can be secured; yet someone could step on the moss or break through it, and then my burrow would lie open, and anybody who liked—please note, however, that quite uncommon abilities would also be required—could make his way in and destroy everything for good. I know that very well, and even now, at the zenith of my life, I can scarcely pass an hour in complete tranquillity; at that one point in the dark moss I am vulnerable, and in my dreams I often see a greedy muzzle sniffing around it persistently. It will be objected that I could quite well have filled in the entrance too, with a thin layer of hard earth on top and with loose soil further down, so that it would not cost me much trouble to dig my way out again whenever I liked. But that plan is impossible; prudence itself demands that I should have a way of leaving at a moment's notice if necessary, prudence itself demands, as alas! so often, to risk one's life. All this involves very laborious calculation, and the sheer pleasure of the mind in its own keenness is often the sole reason why one keeps it up. I must have a way of leaving at a moment's notice, for, despite all my vigilance, may I not be attacked from some quite unexpected quarter? I live in peace in the inmost chamber of my house, and meanwhile the enemy may be burrowing his way slowly and stealthily straight towards me. I do not say that he has a better scent than I; probably he knows as little about me as I of him. But there are insatiable robbers who burrow blindly through the ground, and to whom the very size of my house gives the hope of hitting by chance on some of its far-flung passages. I certainly have the advantage of being in my own house and knowing all the passages and how they run. A robber may very easily become my victim and a succulent one too. But I am growing old; I am not as strong as many others, and my enemies are countless; it could well happen that in flying from one enemy I might run into the jaws of another. Anything might happen! In any case I must have the confident knowledge that somewhere there is an exit easy to reach and quite free, where I have to do nothing whatever to get out, so that I might never—Heaven shield us!—suddenly feel the teeth of the pursuer in my flank while I am desperately burrowing away, even if it is at loose easy soil. And it is not only by external enemies that I am threatened. There are also enemies in the bowels of the earth. I have never seen them, but legend tells of them and I firmly believe in them. They are creatures of the inner earth; not even legend can describe them. Their very victims can scarcely have seen them; they come, you hear the scratching of their claws just under you in the ground, which is their element, and already you are lost. Here it is of no avail to console yourself with the thought that you are in your own house; far rather are you in theirs. Not even my exit could save me from them; indeed in all probability it would not save me in any case, but rather betray me; yet it is a hope, and I cannot live without it. Apart from this main exit I am also connected with the outer world by quite narrow, tolerably safe passages which provide me with good fresh air to breathe. They are the work of the field mice. I have made judicious use of them, transforming them into an organic part of my burrow. They also give me the possibility of scenting things from afar, and thus serve as a protection. All sorts of small fry, too, come running through them, and I devour these; so I can have a certain amount of subterranean hunting, sufficient for a modest way of life, without leaving my burrow at all; and that is naturally a great advantage.

But the most beautiful thing about my burrow is the stillness. Of course, that is deceptive. At any moment it may be shattered and then all will be over. For the time being, however, the silence is still with me. For hours I can stroll through my passages and hear nothing except the rustling of some little creature, which I immediately reduce to silence between my jaws, or the pattering of soil, which draws my attention to the need for repair; otherwise all is still. The fragrance of the woods floats in; the place feels both warm and cool. Sometimes I lie down and roll about in the passage with pure joy. When autumn sets in, to possess a burrow like mine, and a roof over your head, is great good fortune for anyone getting on in years. Every hundred yards I have widened the passages into little round cells; there I can curl myself up in comfort and lie warm. There I sleep the sweet sleep of tranquillity, of satis-

fied desire, of achieved ambition; for I possess a house. I do
not know whether it is a habit that still persists from former
days, or whether the perils even of this house of mine are
great enough to awaken me; but invariably every now and
then I start up out of profound sleep and listen, listen into
the stillness which reigns here unchanged day and night, smile
contentedly and then sink with loosened limbs into still profounder sleep. Poor homeless wanderers in the roads and
woods, creeping for warmth into a heap of leaves or a herd
of their comrades, delivered to all the perils of heaven and
earth! I lie here in a room secured on every side—there are
more than fifty such rooms in my burrow—and pass as much
of my time as I choose between dozing and unconscious
sleep.

Not quite in the center of the burrow, carefully chosen to
serve as a refuge in case of extreme danger from siege if not
from immediate pursuit, lies the chief cell. While all the rest
of the burrow is the outcome rather of intense intellectual
than of physical labor, this Castle Keep was fashioned by the
most arduous labor of my whole body. Several times, in the
despair brought on by physical exhaustion, I was on the point
of giving up the whole business, flung myself down panting
and cursed the burrow, dragged myself outside and left the
place lying open to all the world. I could afford to do that,
for I had no longer any wish to return to it, until at last, after
four hours or days, back I went repentantly, and when I saw
that the burrow was unharmed I could almost have raised
a hymn of thanksgiving, and in sincere gladness of heart started
on the work anew. My labors on the Castle Keep were also
made harder, and unnecessarily so (unnecessarily in that the
burrow derived no real benefit from those labors) by the fact
that just at the place where, according to my calculations,
the Castle Keep should be, the soil was very loose and sandy
and had literally to be hammered and pounded into a firm
state to serve as a wall for the beautifully vaulted chamber.

But for such tasks the only tool I possess is my forehead. So I had to run with my forehead thousands and thousands of times, for whole days and nights, against the ground, and I was glad when the blood came, for that was a proof that the walls were beginning to harden; and in that way, as everybody must admit, I richly paid for my Castle Keep.

In the Castle Keep I assemble my stores; everything over and above my daily wants that I capture inside the burrow, and everything I bring back with me from my hunting expeditions outside, I pile up here. The place is so spacious that food for half a year scarcely fills it. Consequently I can divide up my stores, walk about among them, play with them, enjoy their plenty and their various smells, and reckon up exactly how much they represent. That done, I can always arrange accordingly, and make my calculations and hunting plans for the future, taking into account the season of the year. There are times when I am so well provided for that in my indifference to food I never even touch the smaller fry that scuttle about the burrow, which, however, is probably imprudent of me. My constant preoccupation with defensive measures involves a frequent alteration or modification, though within narrow limits, of my views on how the building can best be organized for that end. Then it sometimes seems risky to make the Castle Keep the basis of defense; the ramifications of the burrow present me with manifold possibilities, and it seems more in accordance with prudence to divide up my stores somewhat, and put part of them in certain of the smaller rooms; thereupon I mark off every third room, let us say, as a reserve storeroom, or every fourth room as a main and every second as an auxiliary storeroom, and so forth. Or I ignore certain passages altogether and store no food in them, so as to throw any enemy off the scent, or I choose quite at random a very few rooms according to their distance from the main exit. Each of these new plans involves of course heavy work; I have to make my calculations and then carry my stores to their new places. True, I can do that at my leisure and without any hurry, and it is not at all unpleasant to carry such good food in your jaws, to lie down and rest whenever you like, and to nibble an occasional tasty tidbit. But it is not so pleasant when, as sometimes happens, you suddenly fancy, starting up from your sleep, that the present distribution of your stores is completely and totally wrong, might lead to great dangers, and must be set right at once, no matter how tired or sleepy you may be; then I rush, then I fly, then I have no time for calculation; and although I was about to execute a perfectly new, perfectly exact plan, I now seize whatever my teeth hit upon and drag it or carry it away, sighing, groaning, stumbling, and even the most haphazard change in the present situation, which seems so terribly dangerous, can satisfy me. Until little by little full wakefulness sobers me, and I can hardly understand my panic haste, breathe in deeply the tranquillity of my house, which I myself have disturbed, return to my resting place, fall asleep at once in a new-won exhaustion, and on awakening find hanging from my jaws, say, a rat, as indubitable proof of night labors which already seem almost unreal. Then again there are times when the storing of all my food in one place seems the best plan of all. Of what use to me could my stores in the smaller rooms be, how much could I store there in any case? And whatever I put there would block the passage, and be a greater hindrance than help to me if I were pursued and had to fly. Besides, it is stupid but true that one's self-conceit suffers if one cannot see all one's stores together, and so at one glance know how much one possesses. And in dividing up my food in those various ways might not a great deal get lost? I can't be always scouring through all my passages and cross-passages so as to make sure that everything is in order. The idea of dividing up my stores is of course a good one, but only if one had several rooms similar to my Castle Keep. Several such rooms! Indeed! And who is to build them? In any case, they could not be worked into the general plan of my burrow at this late stage. But I will admit that that is a fault in my burrow; it is always a fault to have only one piece of anything. And I confess too that during the whole time I was constructing the burrow a vague idea that I should have more such cells stirred in my mind, vaguely, yet clearly enough if I had only welcomed it; I did not yield to it, I felt too feeble for the enormous labor it would involve, more, I felt too feeble even to admit to myself the necessity for that labor, and comforted myself as best I could with the vague hope that a building which in any other case would clearly be inadequate, would in my own unique, exceptional, favored case suffice, presumably because providence was interested in the preservation of my forehead, that unique instrument. So I have only one Castle Keep, but my dark premonitions that one would not suffice have faded. However that may be, I must content myself with the one big chamber, the smaller ones are simply no substitute for it, and so, when this conviction has grown on me, I begin once more to haul all my stores back from them to the Castle Keep. For some time afterwards I find a certain comfort in having all the passages and rooms free, in seeing my stores growing in the Castle Keep and emitting their variegated and mingled smells, each of which delights me in its own fashion, and every one of which I can distinguish even at a distance, as far as the very remotest passages. Then I usually enjoy periods of particular tranquillity, in which I change my sleeping place by stages, always working in towards the center of the burrow, always steeping myself more profoundly in the mingled smells, until at last I can no longer restrain myself and one night rush into the Castle Keep, mightily fling myself upon my stores, and glut myself with the best that I can seize until I am completely gorged. Happy but dangerous hours; anyone who knew how to exploit them could destroy me with ease and without any risk. Here too the absence of a second or third large storeroom works to my detriment; for it is the single huge accumulated mass of food that seduces me. I try to guard myself in various ways against this danger; the distribution of my stores in the smaller rooms is really one of these expedients; but unfortunately, like other such expedients, it leads through renunciation to still greater greed, which, overruling my intelligence, makes me arbitrarily alter my plans of defense to suit its ends.

To regain my composure after such lapses I make a practice of reviewing the burrow, and after the necessary improvements have been carried out, frequently leave it, though only for a short spell. Even at such moments the hardship of being without it for a long time seems too punitive to me, yet I recognize clearly the need for occasional short excursions. It is always with a certain solemnity that I approach the exit again. During my spells of home life I avoid it, steer clear even of the outer windings of the corridor that leads to it; besides, it is no easy job to wander about out there, for I have contrived there a whole little maze of passages; it was there that I began my burrow, at a time when I had no hope of ever completing it according to my plans; I began, half in play, at that corner, and so my first joy in labor found riotous satisfaction there in a labyrinthine burrow which at the time seemed to me the crown of all burrows, but which I judge today, perhaps with more justice, to be too much of an idle *tour de force*, not really worthy of the rest of the burrow, and though perhaps theoretically brilliant—here is my main entrance, I said in those days, ironically addressing my invisible enemies and seeing them all already caught and stifled in the outer labyrinth—is in reality a flimsy piece of jugglery that would hardly withstand a serious attack or the struggles of an enemy fighting for his life. Should I reconstruct this part of my burrow? I keep on postponing the decision, and the labyrinth will probably remain as it is. Apart from the sheer hard work that I should have to face, the task would also be the most dangerous imaginable. When I began the burrow

I could work away at it in comparative peace of mind, the risk wasn't much greater than any other risk; but to attempt that today would be to draw the whole world's attention, and gratuitously, to my burrow; today the whole thing is impossible. I am almost glad of that, for I still have a certain sentiment about this first achievement of mine. And if a serious attack were attempted, what pattern of entrance at all would be likely to save me? An entrance can deceive, can lead astray, can give the attacker no end of worry, and the present one too can do that at a pinch. But a really serious attack has to be met by an instantaneous mobilization of all the resources in the burrow and all the forces of my body and soul—that is self-evident. So this entrance can very well remain where it is. The burrow has so many unavoidable defects imposed by natural causes that it can surely stand this one defect for which I am responsible, and which I recognize as a defect, even if only after the event. In spite of that, however, I do not deny that this fault worries me from time to time, indeed always. If on my customary rounds I avoid this part of the burrow, the fundamental reason is that the sight of it is painful to me, because I don't want to be perpetually reminded of a defect in my house, even if that defect is only too disturbingly present in my mind. Let it continue to exist ineradicably at the entrance; I can at least refuse to look at it as long as that is possible. If I merely walk in the direction of the entrance, even though I may be separated from it by several passages and rooms, I find myself sensing an atmosphere of great danger, actually as if my hair were growing thin and in a moment might fly off and leave me bare and shivering, exposed to the howls of my enemies. Yes, the mere thought of the door itself, the end of the domestic protection, brings such feelings with it, yet it is the labyrinth leading up to it that torments me most of all. Sometimes I dream that I have reconstructed it, transformed it completely, quickly, in a night, with a giant's strength, nobody having noticed, and now it is impregnable; the nights in which such dreams come to me are the sweetest I know, tears of joy and deliverance still glisten on my beard when I awaken.

So I must thread the tormenting complications of this labyrinth physically as well as mentally whenever I go out, and I am both exasperated and touched when, as sometimes happens, I lose myself for a moment in my own maze, and the work of my hands seems to be still doing its best to prove its sufficiency to me, its maker, whose final judgment has long since been passed on it. But then I find myself beneath the mossy covering, which has been left untouched for so long— for I stay for long spells in my house—that it has grown fast to the soil around it, and now only a little push with my head is needed and I am in the upper world. For a long time I do not dare to make that little movement, and if it were not that I would have to traverse the labyrinth once more, I would certainly leave the matter for the time being and turn back again. Just think. Your house is protected and self-sufficient. You live in peace, warm, well-nourished, master, sole master of all your manifold passages and rooms, and all this you are prepared—not to give up, of course—but to risk it, so to speak; you nurse the confident hope, certainly, that you will regain it; yet is it not a dangerous, a far too dangerous stake that you are playing for? Can there be any reasonable grounds for such a step? No, for such acts as these there can be no reasonable grounds. But all the same, I then cautiously raise the trap door and slip outside, let it softly fall back again, and fly as fast as I can from the treacherous spot.

Yet I am not really free. True, I am no longer confined by narrow passages, but hunt through the open woods, and feel new powers awakening in my body for which there was no room, as it were, in the burrow, not even in the Castle Keep, though it had been ten times as big. The food too is better up here; though hunting is more difficult, success more rare, the results are more valuable from every point of

view; I do not deny all this; I appreciate it and take advantage
of it at least as fully as anyone else, and probably more fully,
for I do not hunt like a vagrant out of mere idleness or des-
peration, but calmly and methodically. Also I am not perma-
nently doomed to this free life, for I know that my term is
measured, that I do not have to hunt here forever, and that,
whenever I am weary of this life and wish to leave it, Someone, whose invitation I shall not be able to withstand, will,
so to speak, summon me to him. And so I can pass my time
here quite without care and in complete enjoyment, or rather
I could, and yet I cannot. My burrow takes up too much of
my thoughts. I fled from the entrance fast enough, but soon
I am back at it again. I seek out a good hiding place and keep
watch on the entrance of my house—this time from outside
—for whole days and nights. Call it foolish if you like; it gives
me infinite pleasure and reassures me. At such times it is as
if I were not so much looking at my house as at myself sleeping, and had the joy of being in a profound slumber and simultaneously of keeping vigilant guard over myself. I am privi-
leged, as it were, not only to dream about the specters of the
night in all the helplessness and blind trust of sleep, but also
at the same time to confront them in actuality with the calm
judgment of the fully awake. And strangely enough I discover
that my situation is not so bad as I had often thought, and
will probably think again when I return to my house. In this
connection—it may be in others too, but in this one especially
—these excursions of mine are truly indispensable. Carefully as
I have chosen an out-of-the-way place for my door, the traffic
that passes it is nevertheless, if one takes a week's observation,
very great; but so it is, no doubt, in all inhabited regions, and
probably it is actually better to hazard the risks of dense traffic,
whose very impetus carries it past, than to be delivered in
complete solitude to the first persistently searching intruder.
Here enemies are numerous and their allies and accomplices
still more numerous, but they fight one another, and while thus

employed rush past my burrow without noticing it. In all my time I have never seen anyone investigating the actual door of my house, which is fortunate both for me and for him, for I would certainly have launched myself at his throat, forgetting everything else in my anxiety for the burrow. True, creatures come, in whose vicinity I dare not remain, and from whom I have to fly as soon as I scent them in the distance; on their attitude to the burrow I really can't pronounce with certainty, but it is at least a reassurance that when I presently return I never find any of them there, and the entrance is undamaged. There have been happy periods in which I could almost assure myself that the enmity of the world towards me had ceased or been assuaged, or that the strength of the burrow had raised me above the destructive struggle of former times. The burrow has probably protected me in more ways than I thought or dared think while I was inside it. This fancy used to have such a hold over me that sometimes I have been seized by the childish desire never to return to the burrow again, but to settle down somewhere close to the entrance, to pass my life watching the entrance, and gloat perpetually upon the reflection—and in that find my happiness—how steadfast a protection my burrow would be if I were inside it. Well, one is soon roughly awakened from childish dreams. What does this protection which I am looking at here from the outside amount to after all? Dare I estimate the danger which I run inside the burrow from observations which I make when outside? Can my enemies, to begin with, have any proper awareness of me if I am not in my burrow? A certain awareness of me they certainly have, but not full awareness. And is not that full awareness the real definition of a state of danger? So the experiments I attempt here are only half-experiments or even less, calculated merely to reassure my fears and by giving me false reassurance to lay me open to great perils. No, I do not watch over my own sleep, as I imagined; rather it is I who sleep, while the destroyer watches. Perhaps he is one of those

who pass the entrance without seeming to notice it, concerned
merely to ascertain, just like myself, that the door is still untouched and waits for their attack, and only pass because they
know that the master of the house is out, or because they are
quite aware that he is guilelessly lying on the watch in the
bushes close by. And I leave my post of observation and find
I have had enough of this outside life; I feel that there is
nothing more that I can learn here, either now or at any time.
And I long to say a last goodbye to everything up here, to
go down into my burrow never to return again, let things take
their course, and not try to retard them with my profitless
vigils. But spoilt by seeing for such a long time everything
that happened around the entrance, I find great difficulty in
summoning the resolution to carry out the actual descent,
which might easily draw anyone's attention, and without
knowing what is happening behind my back and behind the
door after it is fastened. I take advantage of stormy nights to
get over the necessary preliminaries, and quickly bundle in my
spoil; that seems to have come off, but whether it has really
come off will only be known when I myself have made the
descent; it will be known, but not by me, or by me, but too
late. So I give up the attempt and do not make the descent. I
dig an experimental burrow, naturally at a good distance from
the real entrance, a burrow just as long as myself, and seal it
also with a covering of moss. I creep into my hole, close it
after me, wait patiently, keep vigil for long or short spells,
and at various hours of the day, then fling off the moss, issue
from my hole, and summarize my observations. These are
extremely heterogeneous, and both good and bad; but I have
never been able to discover a universal principle or an infallible method of descent. In consequence of all this I have not
yet summoned the resolution to make my actual descent, and
am thrown into despair at the necessity of doing it soon. I
almost screw myself to the point of deciding to emigrate to
distant parts and take up my old comfortless life again, which

had no security whatever, but was one indiscriminate succession of perils, yet in consequence prevented one from perceiving and fearing particular perils, as I am constantly reminded by comparing my secure burrow with ordinary life. Certainly such a decision would be an arrant piece of folly, produced simply by living too long in senseless freedom; the burrow is still mine, I have only to take a single step and I am safe. And I tear myself free from all my doubts and by broad daylight rush to the door, quite resolved to raise it now; but I cannot, I rush past it and fling myself into a thorn bush, deliberately, as a punishment, a punishment for some sin I do not know of. Then, at the last moment, I am forced to admit to myself that I was right after all, and that it was really impossible to go down into the burrow without exposing the thing I love best, for a little while at least, to all my enemies, on the ground, in the trees, in the air. And the danger is by no means a fanciful one, but very real. It need not be any particular enemy that is provoked to pursue me, it may very well be some chance innocent little creature, some disgusting little beast which follows me out of curiosity, and thus, without knowing it, becomes the leader of all the world against me; nor need it be even that, it may be—and that would be just as bad, indeed in some respects worse—it may be someone of my own kind, a connoisseur and prizer of burrows, a hermit, a lover of peace, but all the same a filthy scoundrel who wishes to be housed where he has not built. If he were actually to arrive now, if in his obscene lust he were to discover the entrance and set about working at it, lifting the moss; if he were actually to succeed, if he were actually to wriggle his way in in my stead, until only his hindquarters still showed; if all this were actually to happen, so that at last, casting all prudence to the winds, I might in my blind rage leap on him, maul him, tear the flesh from his bones, destroy him, drink his blood and fling his corpse among the rest of my spoil, but above all—that is the main thing

—were at last back in my burrow once more, I would have it in my heart to greet the labyrinth itself with rapture; but first I would draw the moss covering over me, and I would want to rest, it seems to me, for all the remainder of my life. But nobody comes and I am left to my own resources. Perpetually obsessed by the sheer difficulty of the attempt, I lose much of my timidity, I no longer attempt even to appear to avoid the entrance, but make a hobby of prowling around it; by now it is almost as if I were the enemy spying out a suitable opportunity for successfully breaking in. If I only had someone I could trust to keep watch at my post of observation; then of course I could descend in perfect peace of mind. I would make an agreement with this trusty confederate of mine that he would keep a careful note of the state of things during my descent and for quite a long time afterwards, and if he saw any sign of danger knock on the moss covering, and if he saw nothing do nothing. With that a clean sweep would be made of all my fears, no residue would be left, or at most my confidant. For would he not demand some counter-service from me; would he not at least want to see the burrow? That in itself, to let anyone freely into my burrow, would be exquisitely painful to me. I built it for myself, not for visitors, and I think I would refuse to admit him, not even though he alone made it possible for me to get into the burrow would I let him in. But I simply could not admit him, for either I must let him go in first by himself, which is simply unimaginable, or we must both descend at the same time, in which case the advantage I am supposed to derive from him, that of being kept watch over, would be lost. And what trust can I really put in him? Can I trust one whom I have had under my eyes just as fully when I can't see him, and the moss covering separates us? It is comparatively easy to trust anyone if you are supervising him or at least can supervise him; perhaps it is possible even to trust someone at a distance; but completely to trust someone outside the burrow when you are inside the burrow, that is, in a different world, that, it seems to me, is impossible. But such considerations are not in the least necessary; the mere reflection is enough that during or after my descent one of the countless accidents of existence might prevent my confidant from fulfilling his duty, and what incalculable results might not the smallest accident of that kind have for me? No, if one takes it by and large, I have no right to complain that I am alone and have nobody that I can trust. I certainly lose nothing by that and probably spare myself trouble. I can only trust myself and my burrow. I should have thought of that before and taken measures to meet the difficulty that worries me so much now. When I began the burrow it would at least have been partly possible. I should have so constructed the first passage that it had two entrances at a moderate distance from each other, so that after descending through the one entrance with that slowness which is unavoidable, I might rush at once through the passage to the second entrance, slightly raise the moss covering, which would be so arranged as to make that easy, and from there keep watch on the position for several days and nights. That would have been the only right way of doing it. True, the two entrances would double the risk, but that consideration need not delay me, for one of the entrances, serving merely as a post of observation, could be quite narrow. And with that I lose myself in a maze of technical speculations, I begin once more to dream my dream of a completely perfect burrow, and that somewhat calms me; with closed eyes I behold with delight perfect or almost perfect structural devices for enabling me to slip out and in unobserved. While I lie there thinking such things I admire these devices very greatly, but only as technical achievements, not as real advantages; for this freedom to slip out and in at will, what does it amount to? It is the mark of a restless nature, of inner uncertainty, disreputable desires, evil propensities that seem still worse when one thinks of the burrow, which is there at one's hand and can flood one with peace if one only remains quite open and receptive to it. For the present, however, I am out-side it seeking some possibility of returning, and for that the necessary technical devices would be very desirable. But per-haps not so very desirable after all. Is it not a very grave in-justice to the burrow to regard it in moments of nervous panic as a mere hole into which one can creep and be safe? Certainly it is a hole among other things, and a safe one, or should be, and when I picture myself in the midst of danger, then I insist with clenched teeth and all my will that the burrow should be nothing but a hole set apart to save me, and that it should fulfill that clearly defined function with the greatest possible efficiency, and I am ready to absolve it from every other duty. Now the truth of the matter—and one has no eye for that in times of great peril, and only by a great effort even in times when danger is threatening—is that in reality the burrow does provide a considerable degree of security, but by no means enough, for is one ever free from anxieties inside it? These anxieties are different from ordinary ones, prouder, richer in content, often long repressed, but in their destructive effects they are perhaps much the same as the anxieties that existence in the outer world gives rise to. Had I constructed the burrow exclusively to assure my safety I would not have been disappointed, it is true; nevertheless the relation between the enormous labor involved and the actual security it would provide, at least insofar as I could feel it and profit by it, would not have been in my favor. It is extremely painful to have to admit such things to onself, but one is forced to do it, confronted by that entrance over there which now literally locks and bars itself against me, the builder and possessor. Yet the burrow is not a mere hole for taking refuge in. When I stand in the Castle Keep surrounded by my piled-up stores, surveying the ten passages which begin there, raised and sunken passages, vertical and rounded passages, wide and narrow passages, as the general plan dictates, and all alike still and empty, ready by their various routes to conduct me to all the other rooms, which are also still and empty—then all thought of mere safety is far from my mind, then I know that here is my castle, which I have wrested from the refractory soil with tooth and claw, with pounding and hammering blows, my castle which can never belong to anyone else, and is so essentially mine that I can calmly accept in it even my enemy's mortal stroke at the final hour, for my blood will ebb away here in my own soil and not be lost. And what but that is the meaning of the blissful hours which I pass, now peacefully slumbering, now happily keeping watch, in these passages, these passages which suit me so well, where one can stretch oneself out in comfort, roll about in childish delight, lie and dream, or sink into blissful sleep. And the smaller rooms, each familiar to me, so familiar that in spite of their complete similarity I can clearly distinguish one from the other with my eyes shut by the mere feel of the wall: they enclose me more peacefully and warmly than a bird is enclosed in its nest. And all, all still and empty.

But if that is the case, why do I hang back? why do I dread the thought of the intruding enemy more than the possibility of never seeing my burrow again? Well, the latter alternative is fortunately an impossibility; there is no need for me even to take thought to know what the burrow means to me; I and the burrow belong so indissolubly together that in spite of all my fears I could make myself quite comfortable out here, and not even need to overcome my repugnance and open the door; I could be quite content to wait here passively, for nothing can part us for long, and somehow or other I shall quite certainly find myself in my burrow again. But on the other hand how much time may pass before then, and how many things may happen in that time, up here no less than down there? And it lies with me solely to curtail that interval and to do what is necessary at once.

And then, too exhausted to be any longer capable of thought, my head hanging, my legs trembling with fatigue, half asleep, feeling my way rather than walking, I approach the entrance, slowly raise the moss covering, slowly descend, leaving the door open in my distraction for a needlessly long time, and presently remember my omission, and get out again to make it good—but what need was there to get out for that? All that was needed was to draw to the moss covering; right; so I creep in again and now at last draw to the moss covering. Only in this state, and in this state alone, can I achieve my descent. So at last I lie down beneath the moss on the top of my bloodstained spoil and can now enjoy my longed-for sleep. Nothing disturbs me, no one has tracked me down, above the moss everything seems to be quiet thus far at least, but even if all were not quiet I question whether I could stop to keep watch now; I have changed my place, I have left the upper world and am in my burrow, and I feel its effect at once. It is a new world, endowing me with new powers, and what I felt as fatigue up there is no longer that here. I have returned from a journey, dog-tired with my wanderings, but the sight of the old house, the thought of all the things that are waiting to be done, the necessity at least to cast a glance at all the rooms, but above all to make my way immediately to the Castle Keep; all this transforms my fatigue into ardent zeal; it is as though at the moment when I set foot in the burrow I had wakened from a long and profound sleep. My first task is a very laborious one and requires all my attention; I mean getting my spoil through the narrow and thin-walled passages of the labyrinth. I shove with all my might, and the work gets done too, but far too slowly for me; to hasten it I drag part of my flesh supply back again and push my way over it and through it; now I have only a portion of my spoil before me and it is easier to make progress; but my road is so blocked by all this flesh in these narrow passages, through which it is not always easy for me to make my way even when I am alone, that I could quite easily smother among my own stores; sometimes I can only rescue myself from their pressure

by eating and drinking a clear space for myself. But the work
of transport is successful, I finish it in quite a reasonable time,
the labyrinth is behind me, I reach an ordinary passage and
breathe freely, push my spoil through a communication passage
into a main passage expressly designed for the purpose, a passage sloping down steeply to the Castle Keep. What is left
to be done is not really work at all; my whole load rolls and
flows down the passage almost of itself. The Castle Keep at
last! At last I can dare to rest. Everything is unchanged, no
great mishap seems to have occurred, the few little defects
that I note at a first glance can soon be repaired; first, however,
I must go my long round of all the passages, but that is no
hardship, that is merely to commune again with friends, as I
often did in the old days or—I am not so very old yet, but
my memory of many things is already quite confused—as I
often did, or as I have often heard that it was done. Now
I begin with the second passage, purposefully slow, now that
I have seen the Castle Keep I have endless time—inside the
burrow I always have endless time—for everything I do there
is good and important and satisfies me somehow. I begin with
the second passage, but break off in the middle and turn
into the third passage and let it take me back again to the
Castle Keep, and now of course I have to begin at the second
passage once more, and so I play with my task and lengthen
it out and smile to myself and enjoy myself and become quite
dazed with all the work in front of me, but never think of
turning aside from it. It is for your sake, ye passages and rooms,
and you, Castle Keep, above all, that I have come back, count-
ing my own life as nothing in the balance, after stupidly trembling for it for so long, and postponing my return to you.
What do I care for danger now that I am with you? You
belong to me, I to you, we are united; what can harm us?
What if my foes should be assembling even now up above
there and their muzzles be preparing to break through the
moss? And with its silence and emptiness the burrow answers

me, confirming my words. But now a feeling of lassitude over-
comes me and in some favorite room I curl myself up tenta-
tively, I have not yet surveyed everything by a long way, though
still resolved to examine everything to the very end; I have
no intention of sleeping here, I have merely yielded to the
temptation of making myself comfortable and pretending
I want to sleep, I merely wish to find out if this is as good
a place for sleeping as it used to be. It is, but it is a better
place for sleep than for waking, and I remain lying where
I am in deep slumber.

I must have slept for a long time. I was only wakened
when I had reached the last light sleep which dissolves of
itself, and it must have been very light, for it was an almost
inaudible whistling noise that wakened me. I recognized
what it was immediately; the small fry, whom I had allowed
far too much latitude, had burrowed a new channel somewhere during my absence, this channel must have chanced
to intersect an older one, the air was caught there, and that
produced the whistling noise. What an indefatigably busy
lot these small fry are, and what a nuisance their diligence
can be! First I shall have to listen at the walls of my passages and locate the place of disturbance by experimental
excavations, and only then will I be able to get rid of the
noise. However, this new channel may be quite welcome as
a further means of ventilation, if it can be fitted into the
plan of the burrow. But after this I shall keep a much
sharper eye on the small fry than I used to; I shall spare
none of them.

As I have a good deal of experience in investigations of
this kind the work probably will not take me long and I
can start upon it at once; there are other jobs awaiting me,
it is true, but this is the most urgent. I must have silence
in my passages. This noise, however, is a comparatively
innocent one; I did not hear it at all when I first arrived,
although it must certainly have been there; I must first feel

quite at home before I could hear it; it is, so to speak, audible only to the ear of the householder. And it is not even constant, as such noises usually are; there are long pauses, obviously caused by stoppages of the current of air. I start on my investigations, but I can't find the right place to begin at, and though I cut a few trenches I do it at random; naturally that has no effect, and the hard work of digging and the still harder work of filling the trenches up again and beating the earth firm is so much labor lost. I don't seem to be getting any nearer to the place where the noise is, it goes on always on the same thin note, with regular pauses, now a sort of whistling, but again like a kind of piping. Now I could leave it to itself for the time being; it is very disturbing, certainly, but there can hardly be any doubt that its origin is what I took it to be at first; so it can scarcely become louder, on the contrary, such noises may quite well— though until now I have never had to wait so long for that to happen—may quite well vanish of themselves in the course of time through the continued labors of these little burrowers; and apart from that, often chance itself puts one on the track of the disturbance, where systematic investigation has failed for a long time. In such ways I comfort myself, and resolve simply to continue my tour of the passages, and visit the rooms, many of which I have not even seen yet since my return, and enjoy myself contemplating the Castle Keep now and then between times; but my anxiety will not let me, and I must go on with my search. These little creatures take up much, far too much, time that could be better employed. In such cases as the present it is usually the technical problem that attracts me; for example, from the noise, which my ear can distinguish in all its finest shades, so that it has a perfectly clear outline to me, I deduce its cause, and now I am on fire to discover whether my conclusion is valid. And with good reason, for as long as that is not established I cannot feel safe, even if it were merely a matter of discovering where a grain of sand that had fallen from one of the walls had rolled to. And a noise such as this is by no means a trifling matter, regarded from that angle. But whether trifling or important, I can find nothing, no matter how hard I search, or it may be that I find too much. This had to happen just in my favorite room, I think to myself, and I walk a fair distance away from it, almost halfway along the passage leading to the next room; I do this more as a joke, pretending to myself that my favorite room is not alone to blame, but that there are disturbances elsewhere as well, and with a smile on my face I begin to listen; but soon I stop smiling, for, right enough, the same whistling meets me here too. It is really nothing to worry about; sometimes I think that nobody but myself would hear it; it is true, I hear it now more and more distinctly, for my ear has grown keener through practice; though in reality it is exactly the same noise wherever I may hear it, as I have convinced myself by comparing my impressions. Nor is it growing louder; I recognize this when I listen in the middle of the passage instead of pressing my ear against the wall. Then it is only with an effort, indeed with great intentness, that I can more guess at than hear the merest trace of a noise now and then. But it is this very uniformity of the noise everywhere that disturbs me most, for it cannot be made to agree with my original asumption. Had I rightly divined the cause of the noise, then it must have issued with greatest force from some given place, which it would be my task to discover, and after that have grown fainter and fainter. But if my hypothesis does not meet the case, what can the explanation be? There still remains the possibility that there are two noises, that up to now I have been listening at a good distance from the two centers, and that while its noise increases, when I draw near to one of them, the total result remains approximately the same for the ear in consequence of the lessening volume of sound from the other center. Already I have almost fancied sometimes, when I have listened carefully, that I could distinguish, if very indistinctly, differences of tone which support this new assumption. In any case I must extend my sphere of investigation much farther than I have done. Accordingly I descend the passage to the Castle Keep and begin to listen there. Strange, the same noise there too. Now it is a noise produced by the burrowing of some species of small fry who have infamously exploited my absence; in any case they have no intention of doing me harm, they are simply busied with their own work, and so long as no obstacle comes in their way they will keep on in the direction they have taken: I know all this, yet that they should have dared to approach the very Castle Keep itself is incomprehensible to me and fills me with agitation, and confuses the faculties which I need so urgently for the work before me. Here I have no wish to discover whether it is the unusual depth at which the Castle Keep lies, or its great extent and correspondingly powerful air suction, calculated to scare burrowing creatures away, or the mere fact that it is the Castle Keep, that by some channel or other has penetrated to their dull minds. In any case, I have never noticed any sign of burrowing in the walls of the Castle Keep until now. Crowds of little beasts have come here, it is true, attracted by the powerful smells; here I have had a constant hunting ground, but my quarry has always burrowed a way through in the upper passages, and come running down here, somewhat fearfully, but unable to withstand such a temptation. But now, it seems, they are burrowing in all the passages. If I had only carried out the best of the grand plans I thought out in my youth and early manhood, or rather, if I had only had the strength to carry them out, for there would have been no lack of will. One of these favorite plans of mine was to isolate the Castle Keep from its surroundings, that is to say, to restrict the thickness of its walls to about my own height, and leave a free space of about the same width all around the Castle Keep, except for a narrow foundation, which un-fortunately would have to be left to bear up the whole. I had always pictured this free space, and not without reason, as the loveliest imaginable haunt. What a joy to lie pressed against the rounded outer wall, pull oneself up, let oneself slide down again, miss one's footing and find oneself on firm earth, and play all those games literally upon the Castle Keep and not inside it; to avoid the Castle Keep, to rest one's eyes from it whenever one wanted, to postpone the joy of seeing it until later and yet not have to do without it, but literally hold it safe between one's claws, a thing that is impossible if you have only an ordinary open entrance to it; but above all to be able to stand guard over it, and in that way to be so completely compensated for renouncing the actual sight of it that, if one had to choose between staying all one's life in the Castle Keep or in the free space outside it, one would choose the latter, content to wander up and down there all one's days and keep guard over the Castle Keep. Then there would be no noises in the walls, no insolent burrowing up to the very Keep itself; then peace would be assured there and I would be its guardian; then I would not have to listen with loathing to the burrowing of the small fry, but with de-light to something that I cannot hear now at all: the mur-murous silence of the Castle Keep.

But that beautiful dream is past and I must set to work, almost glad that now my work has a direct connection with the Castle Keep, for that wings it. Certainly, as I can see more and more clearly, I need all my energies for this task, which at first seemed quite a trifling one. I listen now at the walls of the Castle Keep, and wherever I listen, high or low, at the roof or the floor, at the entrance or in the corners, everywhere, everywhere, I hear the same noise. And how much time, how much care must be wasted in listening to that noise, with its regular pauses. One can, if one wishes, find a tiny deceitful comfort in the fact that here in the

Castle Keep, because of its vastness, one hears nothing at all, as distinguished from the passages, when one stands back from the walls. Simply as a rest and a means to regain my composure I often make this experiment, listen intently and am overjoyed when I hear nothing. But the question still remains, what can have happened? Confronted with this phenomenon my original explanation completely falls to the ground. But I must also reject other explanations which present themselves to me. One could assume, for instance, that the noise I hear is simply that of the small fry themselves at their work. But all my experience contradicts this; I cannot suddenly begin to hear now a thing that I have never heard before though it was always there. My sensitiveness to disturbances in the burrow has perhaps become greater with the years, yet my hearing has by no means grown keener. It is of the very nature of small fry not to be heard. Would I have tolerated them otherwise? Even at the risk of starvation I would have exterminated them. But perhaps—this idea now insinuates itself—I am concerned here with some animal unknown to me. That is possible. True, I have observed the life down here long and carefully enough, but the world is full of diversity and is never wanting in painful surprises. Yet it cannot be a single animal, it must be a whole swarm that has suddenly fallen upon my domain, a huge swarm of little creatures, which as they are audible, must certainly be bigger than the small fry, but yet cannot be very much bigger, for the sound of their labors is itself very faint. It may be, then, a swarm of unknown creatures on their wanderings, who happen to be passing by my way, who disturb me, but will presently cease to do so. So I could really wait for them to pass, and need not put myself to the trouble of work that will be needless in the end. Yet if these creatures are strangers, why is it that I never see any of them? I have already dug a host of trenches, hoping to catch one of them, but I can find not a single one. Then it occurs to me that they may be quite tiny creatures, far tinier than any I am acquainted with, and that it is only the noise they make that is greater. Accordingly I investigate the soil I have dug up, I cast the lumps into the air so that they break into quite small particles, but the noisemakers are not among them. Slowly I come to realize that by digging such small fortuitous trenches I achieve nothing; in doing that I merely disfigure the walls of my burrow, scratching hastily here and there without taking time to fill up the holes again; at many places already there are heaps of earth which block my way and my view. Still, that is only a secondary worry; for now I can neither wander about my house, nor review it, nor rest; often already I have fallen asleep at my work in some hole or other, with one paw clutching the soil above me, from which in a semi-stupor I have been trying to tear a lump. I intend now to alter my methods. I shall dig a wide and carefully constructed trench in the direction of the noise and not cease from digging until, independent of all theories, I find the real cause of the noise. Then I shall eradicate it, if that is within my power, and if it is not, at least I shall know the truth. That truth will bring me either peace or despair, but whether the one or the other, it will be beyond doubt or question. This decision strengthens me. All that I have done till now seems to me far too hasty; in the excitement of my return, while I had not yet shaken myself free from the cares of the upper world, and was not yet completely penetrated by the peace of the burrow, but rather hypersensitive at having had to renounce it for such a long time, I was thrown into complete confusion of mind by an unfamiliar noise. And what was it? A faint whistling, audible only at long intervals, a mere nothing to which I don't say that one could actually get used, for no one could get used to it, but which one could, without actually doing anything about it at once, observe for a while; that is, listen every few hours, let us say, and patiently register the results, instead of, as I had done, keep-

ing one's ear fixed to the wall and at every hint of noise
tearing out a lump of earth, not really hoping to find anything, but simply so as to do something to give expression to
one's inward agitation. All that will be changed now, I hope.
And then, with furious shut eyes, I have to admit to myself
that I hope nothing of the kind, for I am still trembling
with agitation just as I was hours ago, and if my reason did
not restrain me I would probably like nothing better than
to start stubbornly and defiantly digging, simply for the sake
of digging, at some place or other, whether I heard anything
there or not; almost like the small fry, who burrow either
without any object at all or simply because they eat the soil.
My new and reasonable plan both tempts me and leaves me
cold. There is nothing in it to object to, I at least know of no
objection; it is bound, so far as I can see, to achieve my
aim. And yet at bottom I do not believe in it; I believe in
it so little that I do not even fear the terrors which its success may well bring, I do not believe even in a dreadful
denouement; indeed it seems to me that I have been thinking ever since the first appearance of the noise of such a
methodical trench, and have not begun upon it until now
simply because I put no trust in it. In spite of that I shall
of course start on the trench; I have no other alternative; but
I shall not start at once, I shall postpone the task for a little
while. If reason is to be reinstated on the throne, it must
be completely reinstated; I shall not rush blindly into my
task. In any case I shall first repair the damage that I
have done to the burrow with my wild digging; that will
take a good long time, but it is necessary; if the new trench
is really to reach its goal it will probably be long, and if it
should lead to nothing at all it will be endless; in any case
this task means a longish absence from the burrow, though
an absence by no means so painful as an absence in the
upper world, for I can interrupt my work whenever I like
and pay a visit to my house; and even if I should not do that

the air of Castle Keep will be wafted to me and surround me while I work; nevertheless it means leaving the burrow and surrendering myself to an uncertain fate, and consequently I want to leave the burrow in good order behind me; it shall not be said that I, who am fighting for its peace, have myself destroyed that peace without reinstating it at once. So I begin by shovelling the soil back into the holes from which it was taken, a kind of work I am familiar with, that I have done countless times almost without regarding it as work, and at which, particularly as regards the final pressing and smoothing down—and this is no empty boast, but the simple truth—I am unbeatable. But this time everything seems difficult, I am too distracted, every now and then, in the middle of my work, I press my ear to the wall and listen, and without taking any notice let the soil that I have just lifted trickle back into the passage again. The final embellishments, which demand a stricter attention, I can hardly achieve at all. Hideous protuberances, disturbing cracks remain, not to speak of the fact that the old buoyancy simply cannot be restored again to a wall patched up in such a way. I try to comfort myself with the reflection that my present work is only temporary. When I return after peace has been restored I shall repair everything properly: work will be mere play to me then. Oh yes, work is mere play in fairy tales, and this comfort of mine belongs to the realm of fairy tales too. It would be far better to do the work thoroughly now, at once, far more reasonable than perpetually to interrupt it and wander off through the passages to discover new sources of noise, which is easy enough, all that is needed being to stop at any point one likes and listen. And that is not the end of my useless discoveries. Sometimes I fancy that the noise has stopped, for it makes long pauses; sometimes such a faint whistling escapes one, one's own blood is pounding all too loudly in one's ears; then two pauses come one after another, and for a while one thinks that the whistling has stopped forever. I listen no longer, I jump up, all life is transfigured; it is as if the fountains from which flows the silence of the burrow were unsealed. I refrain from verifying my discovery at once, I want first to find someone to whom in all good faith I can confide it, so I rush to the Castle Keep, I remember, for I and everything in me has awakened to new life, that I have eaten nothing for a long time, I snatch something or other from among my store of food half buried under the debris and hurriedly begin to swallow it while I hurry back to the place where I made my incredible discovery, I only want to assure myself about it incidentally, perfunctorily, while I am eating; I listen, but the most perfunctory listening shows at once that I was shamefully deceived: away there in the distance the whistling still remains unshaken. And I spit out my food, and would like to trample it underfoot, and go back to my task, not caring which I take up; any place where it seems to be needed, and there are enough places like that, I mechanically start on something or other, just as if the overseer had appeared and I must make a pretense of working for his benefit. But hardly have I begun to work in this fashion when it may happen that I make a new discovery. The noise seems to have become louder, not much louder, of course—here it is always a matter of the subtlest shades—but all the same sufficiently louder for the ear to recognize it clearly. And this growing-louder is like a coming-nearer; still more distinctly than you hear the increasing loudness of the noise, you can literally see the step that brings it closer to you. You leap back from the wall, you try to grasp at once all the possible consequences that this discovery will bring with it. You feel as if you had never really organized the burrow for defense against attack; you had intended to do so, but despite all your experience of life the danger of an attack, and consequently the need to organize the place for defense, seemed remote—or rather not remote (how could it possibly be!)—but infinitely less important than the need to put it in a state where one could live peacefully; and so that consideration was given priority in everything relating to the burrow. Many things in this direction might have been done without affecting the plan of the whole; most incomprehensibly they have been neglected. I have had a great deal of luck all those years, luck has spoilt me; I have had anxieties, but anxiety leads to nothing when you have luck to back you.

The thing to do, really to do now, would be to go carefully over the burrow and consider every possible means of defending it, work out a plan of defense and a corresponding plan of construction, and then start on the work at once with the vigor of youth. That is the work that would really be needed, for which, I may add, it is now far too late in the day; yet that is what would really be needed, and not the digging of a grand experimental trench, whose only real result would be to deliver me hand and foot to the search for danger, out of the foolish fear that it will not arrive quickly enough of itself. Suddenly I cannot comprehend my former plan. I can find no slightest trace of reason in what had seemed so reasonable; once more I lay aside my work and even my listening;. I have no wish to discover any further signs that the noise is growing louder; I have had enough of discoveries; I let everything slide; I would be quite content if I could only still the conflict going on within me. Once more I let my passages lead me where they will, I come to more and more remote ones that I have not yet seen since my return, and that are quite unsullied by my scratching paws, and whose silence rises up to meet me and sinks into me. I do not surrender to it, I hurry on, I do not know what I want, probably simply to put off the hour. I stray so far that I find myself at the labyrinth; the idea of listening beneath the moss covering tempts me; such distant things, distant for the moment, chain my interest. I push my way up and listen. Deep stillness; how lovely it is

here, outside there nobody troubles about my burrow, everybody has his own affairs, which have no connection with
me; how have I managed to achieve this? Here under the
moss covering is perhaps the only place in my burrow now
where I can listen for hours and hear nothing. A complete
reversal of things in the burrow; what was once the place
of danger has become a place of tranquillity, while the Castle
Keep has been plunged into the melee of the world and all
its perils. Still worse, even here there is no peace in reality,
here nothing has changed; silent or vociferous, danger lies in
ambush as before above the moss, but I have grown insensitive to it, my mind is far too much taken up with the whistling in my walls. Is my mind really taken up with it? It
grows louder, it comes nearer, but I wriggle my way through
the labyrinth and make a couch for myself up here under the
moss; it is almost as if I were already leaving the house to
the whistler, content if I can only have a little peace up here.
To the whistler? Have I come, then, to a new conclusion
concerning the cause of the noise? But surely the noise is
caused by the channels bored by the small fry? Is not that
my considered opinion? It seems to me that I have not
retreated from it thus far. And if the noise is not caused
directly by these channels, it is indirectly. And even if it
should have no connection with them whatever, one is not
at liberty to make *a priori* assumptions, but must wait until
one finds the cause, or it reveals itself. One could play with
hypotheses, of course, even at this stage; for instance, it is
possible that there has been a water burst at some distance
away, and what seems a piping or whistling to me is in reality
a gurgling. But apart from the fact that I have no experience
in that sphere—the groundwater that I found at the start I
drained away at once, and in this sandy soil it has never
returned—apart from this fact the noise is undeniably a
whistling and simply not to be translated into a gurgling.
But what avail all exhortations to be calm; my imagination

will not rest, and I have actually come to believe—it is useless to deny it to myself—that the whistling is made by some
beast, and moreover not by a great many small ones, but
by a single big one. Many signs contradict this. The noise
can be heard everywhere and always at the same strength,
and moreover uniformly, both by day and night. At first,
therefore, one cannot but incline to the hypothesis of a great
number of little animals; but as I must have found some
of them during my digging and I have found nothing, it only
remains for me to assume the existence of a great beast, especially as the things that seem to contradict the hypothesis
are merely things which make the beast, not so much impossible, as merely dangerous beyond all one's powers of
conception. For that reason alone have I resisted this hypothesis. I shall cease from this self-deception. For a long
time already I have played with the idea that the beast can
be heard at such a great distance because it works so furiously;
it burrows as fast through the ground as another can walk
on the open road; the ground still trembles at its burrowing
when it has ceased; this reverberation and the noise of the
boring itself unite into one sound at such a great distance,
and I, as I hear only the last dying ebb of that sound,
hear it always at the same uniform strength. It follows
from this also that the beast is not making for me, seeing that the noise never changes; more likely it has a plan
in view whose purpose I cannot decipher; I merely assume
that the beast—and I make no claim whatever that it knows
of my existence—is encircling me; it has probably made several circles around my burrow already since I began to observe it. The nature of the noise, the piping or whistling,
gives me much food for thought. When I scratch and scrape
in the soil in my own fashion the sound is quite different.
I can explain the whistling only in this way: that the beast's
chief means of burrowing is not its claws, which it probably
employs merely as a secondary resource, but its snout or its

muzzle, which, of course, apart from its enormous strength, must also be fairly sharp at the point. It probably bores its snout into the earth with one mighty push and tears out a great lump; while it is doing that I hear nothing; that is the pause; but then it draws in the air for a new push. This indrawal of its breath, which must be an earthshaking noise, not only because of the beast's strength, but of its haste, its furious lust for work as well: this noise I hear then as a faint whistling. But quite incomprehensible remains the beast's capacity to work without stopping; perhaps the short pauses provide also the opportunity of snatching a moment's rest; but apparently the beast has never yet allowed itself a really long rest, day and night it goes on burrowing, always with the same freshness and vigor, always thinking of its object, which must be achieved with the utmost expedition, and which it has the ability to achieve with ease. Now I could not have foreseen such an opponent. But apart altogether from the beast's peculiar characteristics, what is happening now is only something which I should really have feared all the time, something against which I should have been constantly prepared: the fact that someone would come. By what chance can everything have flowed on so quietly and happily for such a long time? Who can have diverted my enemies from their path, and forced them to make a wide detour around my property? Why have I been spared for so long, only to be delivered to such terrors now? Compared with this, what are all the petty dangers in brooding over which I have spent my life! Had I hoped, as owner of the burrow, to be in a stronger position than any enemy who might chance to appear? But simply by virtue of being owner of this great vulnerable edifice I am obviously defenseless against any serious attack. The joy of possessing it has spoilt me, the vulnerability of the burrow has made me vulnerable; any wound to it hurts me as if I myself were hit. It is precisely this that I should have foreseen; instead of thinking only of my own defense—and how perfunctorily and vainly I have done even that—I should have thought of the defense of the burrow. Above all, provision should have been made for cutting off sections of the burrow, and as many as possible of them, from the endangered sections when they are attacked; this should have been done by means of improvised landslides, calculated to operate at a moment's notice; moreover these should have been so thick, and have provided such an effectual barrier, that the attacker would not even guess that the real burrow only began at the other side. More, these landslides should have been so devised that they not only concealed the burrow, but also entombed the attacker. Not the slightest attempt have I made to carry out such a plan, nothing at all has been done in this direction, I have been as thoughtless as a child, I have passed my manhood's years in childish games, I have done nothing but play even with the thought of danger, I have shirked really taking thought for actual danger. And there has been no lack of warning.

Nothing, of course, approaching the present situation has happened before; nevertheless there was an incident not unlike it when the burrow was only beginning. The main difference between that time and this is simply that the burrow was only beginning then. . . . In those days I was literally nothing more than a humble apprentice, the labyrinth was only sketched out in rough outline, I had already dug a little room, but the proportions and the execution of the walls were sadly bungled; in short, everything was so tentative that it could only be regarded as an experiment, as something which, if one lost patience some day, one could leave behind without much regret. Then one day as I lay on a heap of earth resting from my labors—I have rested far too often from my labors all my life—suddenly I heard a noise in the distance. Being young at the time, I was less frightened than curious. I left my work to look after itself and set myself to listen; I listened and listened, and had no wish to fly up to my moss covering and stretch myself out there so that I might not have to hear. I did listen, at least. I could clearly recognize that the noise came from some kind of burrowing similar to my own; it was somewhat fainter, of course, but how much of that might be put down to the distance one could not tell. I was intensely interested, but otherwise calm and cool. Perhaps I am in somebody else's burrow, I thought to myself, and now the owner is boring his way towards me. If that assumption had proved to be correct I would have gone away, for I have never had any desire for conquest or bloodshed, and begun building somewhere else. But after all I was still young and still without a burrow, so I could remain quite cool. Besides, the further course of the noise brought no real cause for apprehension, except that it was not easy to explain. If whoever was boring there was really making for me, because he had heard me boring, then if he changed his direction, as now actually happened, it could not be told whether he did this because my pause for rest had deprived him of any definite point to make towards, or because —which was more plausible—he had himself changed his plans. But perhaps I had been deceived altogether, and he had never been actually making in my direction; at any rate the noise grew louder for a while as if he were drawing nearer, and being young at that time I probably would not have been displeased to see the burrower suddenly rising from the ground; but nothing of that kind happened, at a certain point the sound of boring began to weaken, it grew fainter and fainter, as if the burrower were gradually diverging from his first route, and suddenly it broke off altogether, as if he had decided now to take the diametrically opposite direction and were making straight away from me into the distance. For a long time I still went on listening for him in the silence, before I returned once more to my work. Now that warning was definite enough, but I soon forgot it, and it scarcely influenced my building plans.

Between that day and this lie my years of maturity, but is it not as if there were no interval at all between them? I still take long rests from my labors and listen at the wall, and the burrower has changed his intention anew, he has turned back, he is returning from his journey, thinking he has given me ample time in the interval to prepare for his reception. But on my side everything is worse prepared for than it was then; the great burrow stands defenseless, and I am no longer a young apprentice, but an old architect, and the powers I still have fail me when the decisive hour comes; yet old as I am it seems to me that I would gladly be still older, so old that I should never be able to rise again from my resting place under the moss. For to be honest I cannot endure the place, I rise up and rush, as if I had filled myself up there with new anxieties instead of peace, down into the house again. What was the state of things the last time I was here? Had the whistling grown fainter? No, it had grown louder. I listen at ten places chosen at random and clearly notice the deception; the whistling is just the same as ever, nothing has altered. Over there, there are no changes, there one is calm and not worried about time; but here every instant frets and gnaws at the listener. I go once more the long road to the Castle Keep, all my surroundings seem filled with agitation, seem to be looking at me, and then look away again so as not to disturb me, yet cannot refrain the very next moment from trying to read the saving solution from my expression. I shake my head, I have not yet found any solution. Nor do I go to the Castle Keep in pursuance of any plan. I pass the spot where I had intended to begin the experimental trench, I look it over once more, it would have been an admirable place to begin at, the trench's course would have been in the direction where lay the majority of

the tiny ventilation holes, which would have greatly lightened
my labors; perhaps I should not have had to dig very far, should
not even have had to dig to the source of the noise; perhaps if I had listened at the ventilation holes it would have
been enough. But no consideration is potent enough to ani-
mate me to this labor of digging. This trench will bring me
certainty, you say? I have reached the stage where I no
longer wish to have certainty. In the Castle Keep I choose a
lovely piece of flayed red flesh and creep with it into one
of the heaps of earth; there I shall have silence at least,
such silence, at any rate, as still can be said to exist here.
I munch and nibble at the flesh, think of the strange
beast going its own road in the distance, and then again that
I should enjoy my store of food as fully as possible, while I
still have the chance. This last is probably the sole plan I
have left that I can carry out. For the rest I try to unriddle
the beast's plans. Is it on its wanderings, or is it working
on its own burrow? If it is on its wanderings then perhaps
an understanding with it might be possible. If it should really
break through to the burrow I shall give it some of my
stores and it will go on its way again. It will go its way again,
a fine story! Lying in my heap of earth I can naturally
dream of all sorts of things, even of an understanding with
the beast, though I know well enough that no such thing
can happen, and that at the instant when we see each other,
more, at the moment when we merely guess at each other's
presence, we shall both blindly bare our claws and teeth,
neither of us a second before or after the other, both of us
filled with a new and different hunger, even if we should
already be gorged to bursting. And with entire justice, for
who, even if he were merely on his wanderings, would not
change his itinerary and his plans for the future on catching
sight of the burrow? But perhaps the beast is digging in its
own burrow, in which case I cannot even dream of an understanding. Even if it should be such a peculiar beast that its

burrow could tolerate a neighbor, my burrow could not
tolerate a neighbor, at least not a clearly audible one. Now
actually the beast seems to be a great distance away; if it
would only withdraw a little farther the noise too would probably disappear; perhaps in that case everything would be
peaceful again as in the old days; all this would then become a painful but salutary lesson, spurring me on to make
the most diverse improvements on the burrow; if I have
peace, and danger does not immediately threaten me, I am
still quite fit for all sorts of hard work; perhaps, considering
the enormous possibilities which its powers of work open
before it, the beast has given up the idea of extending its
burrow in my direction, and is compensating itself for that
in some other one. That consummation also cannot, of
course, be brought about by negotiation, but only by the
beast itself, or by some compulsion exercised from my side.
In both cases the decisive factor will be whether the beast
knows about me, and if so what it knows. The more I reflect
upon it the more improbable does it seem to me that the
beast has even heard me; it is possible, though I can't imagine it, that it can have received news of me in some other
way, but it has certainly never heard me. So long as I still
knew nothing about it, it simply cannot have heard me, for
at that time I kept very quiet, nothing could be more quiet
than my return to the burrow; afterwards, when I dug the
experimental trenches, perhaps it could have heard me,
though my style of digging makes very little noise; but if
it had heard me I must have noticed some sign of it, the
beast must at least have stopped its work every now and then
to listen. But all remained unchanged.

THE GREAT WALL
OF CHINA

THE GREAT WALL OF CHINA was finished off at its northernmost corner. From the southeast and the southwest it came up in two sections that finally converged there. This principle of piecemeal construction was also applied on a smaller scale by both of the two great armies of labor, the eastern and the western. It was done in this way: gangs of some twenty workers were formed who had to accomplish a length, say, of five hundred yards of wall, while a similar gang built another stretch of the same length to meet the first. But after the junction had been made the construction of the wall was not carried on from the point, let us say, where this thousand yards ended; instead the two groups of workers were transferred to begin building again in quite different neighborhoods. Naturally in this way many great gaps were left, which were only filled in gradually and bit by bit, some, indeed, not till after the official announcement that the wall was finished. In fact it is said that there are gaps which have never been filled in at all, an assertion, however, which is probably merely one of the many legends to which the building of the wall gave rise, and which cannot be verified, at least by any single man with his own eyes and judgment, on account of the extent of the structure.

Now on first thoughts one might conceive that it would have been more advantageous in every way to build the wall continuously, or at least continuously within the two main divisions. After all, the wall was intended, as was universally proclaimed and known, to be a protection against the peoples of the north. But how can a wall protect if it is not a continuous structure? Not only can such a wall not protect, but what there is of it is in perpetual danger. These blocks of wall left standing in deserted regions could be easily pulled down again and again by the nomads, especially as these tribes, rendered apprehensive by the building operations, kept changing their encampments with incredible rapidity, like locusts, and so perhaps had a better general view of the progress of the wall than we, the builders. Nevertheless the task of construction probably could not have been carried out in any other way. To understand this we must take into account the following: the wall was to be a protection for centuries; accordingly, the most scrupulous care in the building, the application of the architectural wisdom of all known ages and peoples, an unremitting sense of personal responsibility in the builders were indispensable prerequisites for the work. True, for the more purely manual tasks ignorant day laborers from the populace, men, women and children who offered their services for good money, could be employed; but for the supervision even of every four day laborers an expert versed in the art of building was required, a man who was capable of entering into and feeling with all his heart what was involved. And the higher the task, the greater the responsibility. And such men were actually to be had, if not indeed so abundantly as the work of construction could have absorbed, yet in great numbers.

For the work had not been undertaken without thought. Fifty years before the first stone was laid the art of architecture, and especially that of masonry, had been proclaimed as the most important branch of knowledge throughout the whole area of a China that was to be walled around, and all other arts gained recognition only insofar as they had reference to it. I can still remember quite well us standing as small children, scarcely sure on our feet, in our teacher's garden, and being ordered to build a sort of wall out of pebbles; and then the teacher, girding up his robe, ran full tilt against the wall, of course knocking it down, and scolded us so terribly for the shoddiness of our work that we ran weeping in all directions to our parents. A trivial incident, but significant of the spirit of the time.

I was lucky inasmuch as the building of the wall was just beginning when, at twenty, I had passed the last examination of the lowest school. I say lucky, for many who before my time had achieved the highest degree of culture available to them could find nothing year after year to do with their knowledge, and drifted uselessly about with the most splendid architectural plans in their heads, and sank by thousands into hopelessness. But those who finally came to be employed in the work as supervisors, even though it might be of the lowest rank, were truly worthy of their task. They were masons who had reflected much, and did not cease to reflect, on the building of the wall, men who with the first stone they sank in the ground felt themselves a part of the wall. Masons of that kind, of course, had not only a desire to per· form their work in the most thorough manner, but were also impatient to see the wall finished in its complete perfection. Day laborers have not this impatience, for they look only to their wages, and the higher supervisors, indeed even the supervisors of middle rank, could see enough of the manifold growth of the construction to keep their spirits confident and high. But to encourage the subordinate supervisors, intellectually so vastly superior to their apparently petty tasks, other measures must be taken. One could not, for instance, expect them to lay one stone on another for months or even years on end, in an uninhabited mountainous region, hundreds of miles from their homes; the hopelessness of such hard toil, which yet could not reach completion even in the longest lifetime, would have cast them into despair and above all made them less capable for the work. It was for this reason that the system of piecemeal building was decided on. Five hundred yards could be accomplished in about five years; by that time, however, the supervisors were as a rule quite exhausted and had lost all faith in themselves, in the wall, in the world. Accordingly, while they were still exalted by the jubilant celebrations marking the completion of the thousand yards of wall, they were sent far, far away, saw on their journey finished sections of the wall rising here and there, came past the quarters of the high command and were presented with badges of honor, heard the rejoicings of new armies of labor streaming past from the depths of the land, saw forests being cut down to become supports for the wall, saw mountains being hewn into stones for the wall, heard at the holy shrines hymns rising in which the pious prayed for the completion of the wall. All this assuaged their impatience. The quiet life of their homes, where they rested some time, strengthened them; the humble credulity with which their reports were listened to, the confidence with which the simple and peaceful burgher believed in the eventual completion of the wall, all this filled their hearts with a new buoyancy. Like eternally hopeful children they then said farewell to their homes; the desire once more to labor on the wall of the nation became irresistible. They set off earlier than they needed; half the village accompanied them for long distances. Groups of people with banners and streamers waving were on all the roads; never before had they seen how great and rich and beautiful and worthy of love their country was. Every fellow countryman was a brother for whom one was building a wall of protection, and who would return lifelong thanks for it with all he had and did. Unity! Unity! Shoulder to shoulder, a ring of brothers, a current of blood no longer confined within the narrow circulation of one body, but sweetly rolling and yet ever returning throughout the endless leagues of China.

Thus, then, the system of piecemeal construction becomes comprehensible; but there were still other reasons for it as well. Nor is there anything odd in my pausing over this question for so long; it is one of the crucial problems in the whole building of the wall, unimportant as it may appear at first glance. If I am to convey and make understandable the ideas and feelings of that time I cannot go deeply enough into this very question.

First, then, it must be said that in those days things were achieved scarcely inferior to the construction of the Tower of Babel, although as regards divine approval, at least according to human reckoning, strongly at variance with that work. I say this because during the early days of building a scholar wrote a book in which he drew the comparison in the most exhaustive way. In it he tried to prove that the Tower of Babel failed to reach its goal, not because of the reasons universally advanced, or at least that among those recognized reasons the most important of all was not to be found. His proofs were drawn not merely from written documents and reports; he also claimed to have made inquiries on the spot, and to have discovered that the tower failed and was bound to fail because of the weakness of the foundation. In this respect at any rate our age was vastly superior to that ancient one. Almost every educated man of our time was a mason by profession and infallible in the matter of laying foundations. That, however, was not what our scholar was concerned to prove; for he maintained that the Great Wall alone would provide for the first time in the history of mankind a secure foundation for a new Tower of Babel. First the wall, therefore, and then the tower. His book was in everybody's hands at that time, but I admit that even today I cannot quite make out how he conceived this tower.

How could the wall, which did not form even a circle, but only a sort of quarter- or half-circle, provide the foundation for a tower? That could obviously be meant only in a spiritual sense. But in that case why build the actual wall, which after all was something concrete, the result of the lifelong labor of multitudes of people? And why were there in the book plans, somewhat nebulous plans, it must be admitted, of the tower, and proposals worked out in detail for mobilizing the people's energies for the stupendous new work?

There were many wild ideas in people's heads at that time —this scholar's book is only one example—perhaps simply because so many were trying to join forces as far as they could for the achievement of a single aim. Human nature, essentially changeable, unstable as the dust, can endure no restraint; if it binds itself it soon begins to tear madly at its bonds, until it rends everything asunder, the wall, the bonds and its very self.

It is possible that these very considerations, which militated against the building of the wall at all, were not left out of account by the high command when the system of piecemeal construction was decided on. We—and here I speak in the name of many people—did not really know ourselves until we had carefully scrutinized the decrees of the high command, when we discovered that without the high command neither our book learning nor our human understanding would have sufficed for the humble tasks which we performed in the great whole. In the office of the command —where it was and who sat there no one whom I have asked knew then or knows now—in that office one may be certain that all human thoughts and desires revolved in a circle, and all human aims and fulfillments in a countercircle. And through the window the reflected splendors of divine worlds fell on the hands of the leaders as they traced their plans.

And for that reason the incorruptible observer must hold that the command, if it had seriously desired it, could also

have overcome those difficulties which prevented a system
of continuous construction. There remains, therefore, nothing
but the conclusion that the command deliberately chose the
system of piecemeal construction. But the piecemeal construction was only a makeshift and therefore inexpedient. Remains the conclusion that the command willed something
inexpedient. Strange conclusion! True, and yet in one respect
it has much to be said for it. One can perhaps safely discuss it now. In those days many people, and among them
the best, had a secret maxim which ran: Try with all your
might to comprehend the decrees of the high command, but
only up to a certain point; then avoid further meditation.
A very wise maxim, which moreover was elaborated in a parable that was later often quoted: Avoid further meditation,
but not because it might be harmful; it is not at all certain
that it would be harmful. What is harmful or not harmful
has nothing to do with the question. Consider rather the
river in spring. It rises until it grows mightier and nourishes
more richly the soil on the long stretch of its banks, still
maintaining its own course until it reaches the sea, where it
is all the more welcome because it is a worthier ally. Thus
far may you urge your meditations on the decrees of the
high command. But after that the river overflows its banks,
loses outline and shape, slows down the speed of its current,
tries to ignore its destiny by forming little seas in the interior
of the land, damages the fields, and yet cannot maintain
itself for long in its new expanse, but must run back between
its banks again, must even dry up wretchedly in the hot
season that presently follows. Thus far may you not urge your
meditations on the decrees of the high command.

Now though this parable may have had extraordinary point
and force during the building of the wall, it has at most only
a restricted relevance for my present essay. My inquiry is
purely historical; no lightning flashes any longer from the
long since vanished thunderclouds, and so I may venture to

seek for an explanation of the system of piecemeal construction which goes farther than the one that contented people then. The limits which my capacity for thought imposes upon me are narrow enough, but the province to be traversed here is infinite.

Against whom was the Great Wall to serve as a protection? Against the people of the north. Now, I come from the southeast of China. No northern people can menace us there. We read of them in the books of the ancients; the cruelties they commit in accordance with their nature make us sigh in our peaceful arbors. The faithful representations of the artist show us these faces of the damned, their gaping mouths, their jaws furnished with great pointed teeth, their half-shut eyes that already seem to be seeking out the victim which their jaws will rend and devour. When our children are unruly we show them these pictures, and at once they fly weeping into our arms. But nothing more than that do we know about these northerners. We have not seen them, and if we remain in our villages we shall never see them, even if on their wild horses they should ride as hard as they can straight towards us—the land is too vast and would not let them reach us, they would end their course in the empty air.

Why, then, since that is so, did we leave our homes, the stream with its bridges, our mothers and fathers, our weeping wives, our children who needed our care, and depart for the distant city to be trained there, while our thoughts journeyed still farther away to the wall in the north? Why? A question for the high command. Our leaders know us. They, absorbed in gigantic anxieties, know of us, know our petty pursuits, see us sitting together in our humble huts, and approve or disapprove the evening prayer which the father of the house recites in the midst of his family. And if I may be allowed to express such ideas about the high command, then I must say that in my opinion the high command has existed from old time, and was not assembled, say, like a gathering of mandarins summoned hastily to discuss somebody's fine dream in a conference as hastily terminated, so that that very evening the people are drummed out of their beds to carry out what has been decided, even if it should be nothing but an illumination in honor of a god who may have shown great favor to their masters the day before, only to drive them into some dark corner with cudgel blows tomorrow, almost before the illuminations have died down. Far rather do I believe that the high command has existed from all eternity, and the decision to build the wall likewise. Unwitting peoples of the north, who imagined they were the cause of it! Honest, unwitting Emperor, who imagined he decreed it! We builders of the wall know that it was not so and hold our tongues.

During the building of the wall and ever since to this very day I have occupied myself almost exclusively with the comparative history of races—there are certain questions which one can probe to the marrow, as it were, only by this method —and I have discovered that we Chinese possess certain folk and political institutions that are unique in their clarity, others again unique in their obscurity. The desire to trace the cause of these phenomena, especially the latter, has always intrigued me and intrigues me still, and the building of the wall is itself essentially involved with these problems.

Now one of the most obscure of our institutions is that of the empire itself. In Peking, naturally, at the imperial court, there is some clarity to be found on this subject, though even that is more illusive than real. Also the teachers of political law and history in the schools of higher learning claim to be exactly informed on these matters, and to be capable of passing on their knowledge to their students. The farther one descends among the lower schools the more, naturally enough, does one find teachers' and pupils' doubts of their own knowledge vanishing, and superficial culture mounting sky-high around a few precepts that have been drilled into people's minds for centuries, precepts which, though they have lost nothing of their eternal truth, remain eternally invisible in this fog of confusion.

But it is precisely this question of the empire which in my opinion the common people should be asked to answer, since after all they are the empire's final support. Here, I must confess, I can only speak once more for my native place. Except for the nature gods, and their ritual which fills the whole year in such beautiful and rich alternation, we think only about the Emperor. But not about the present one; or rather we would think about the present one if we knew who he was or knew anything definite about him. True—and it is the sole curiosity that fills us—we are always trying to get information on this subject, but, strange as it may sound, it is almost impossible to discover anything, either from pilgrims, though they have wandered through much of our land, or from near or distant villages, or from sailors, though they have navigated not only our little stream, but also the sacred rivers. One hears a great many things, true, but can gather nothing definite.

So vast is our land that no fable could do justice to its vastness, the heavens can scarcely span it—and Peking is only a dot in it, and the imperial palace less than a dot. The Emperor as such, on the other hand, is mighty throughout all the hierarchies of the world: admitted. But the existent Emperor, a man like us, lies much like us on a couch which is of generous proportions, perhaps, and yet very possibly may be quite narrow and short. Like us he sometimes stretches himself and when he is very tired yawns with his delicately cut mouth. But how should we know anything about that—thousands of miles away in the south—almost on the borders of the Tibetan Highlands? And besides, any tidings, even if they did reach us, would arrive far too late, would have become obsolete long before they reached us. The Emperor is always surrounded by a brilliant and yet

ambiguous throng of nobles and courtiers—malice and enmity in the guise of servants and friends—who form a coun-
terweight to the imperial power and perpetually labor to
unseat the ruler from his place with poisoned arrows. The
Empire is immortal, but the Emperor himself totters and falls
from his throne, yes, whole dynasties sink in the end and
breathe their last in one death rattle. Of these struggles and
sufferings the people will never know; like tardy arrivals, like
strangers in a city, they stand at the end of some densely
thronged sidestreet peacefully munching the food they have
brought with them, while far away in front, in the market
square at the heart of the city, the execution of their ruler
is proceeding.

There is a parable that describes this situation very well:
The Emperor, so it runs, has sent a message to you, the
humble subject, the insignificant shadow cowering in the
remotest distance before the imperial sun; the Emperor from
his deathbed has sent a message to you alone. He has commanded the messenger to kneel down by the bed, and has
whispered the message to him; so much store did he lay on
it that he ordered the messenger to whisper it back into his
ear again. Then by a nod of the head he has confirmed that
it is right. Yes, before the assembled spectators of his death
—all the obstructing walls have been broken down, and on
the spacious and loftily mounting open staircases stand in a
ring the great princes of the Empire—before all these he has
delivered his message. The messenger immediately sets out on
his journey; a powerful, an indefatigable man; now pushing
with his right arm, now with his left, he cleaves a way for
himself through the throng; if he encounters resistance he
points to his breast, where the symbol of the sun glitters;
the way is made easier for him than it would be for any other
man. But the multitudes are so vast; their numbers have no
end. If he could reach the open fields how fast he would
fly, and soon doubtless you would hear the welcome hammer-

ing of his fists on your door. But instead how vainly does he wear out his strength; still he is only making his way through the chambers of the innermost palace; never will he get to the end of them; and if he succeeded in that nothing would be gained; he must next fight his way down the stair; and if he succeeded in that nothing would be gained; the courts would still have to be crossed; and after the courts the second outer palace; and once more stairs and courts; and once more another palace; and so on for thousands of years; and if at last he should burst through the outermost gate—but never, never can that happen—the imperial capital would lie before him, the center of the world, crammed to bursting with its own sediment. Nobody could fight his way through here even with a message from a dead man. But you sit at your window when evening falls and dream it to yourself.

Just so, as hopelessly and as hopefully, do our people regard the Emperor. They do not know what Emperor is reigning, and there exist doubts regarding even the name of the dynasty. In school a great deal is taught about the dynasties with the dates of succession, but the universal uncertainty in this matter is so great that even the best scholars are drawn into it. Long-dead emperors are set on the throne in our villages, and one that only lives on in song recently had a proclamation of his read out by the priest before the altar. Battles that are old history are new to us, and one's neighbor rushes in with a jubilant face to tell the news. The wives of the emperors, pampered and overweening, seduced from noble custom by wily courtiers, swelling with ambition, vehement in their greed, uncontrollable in their lust, practice their abominations ever anew. The more deeply they are buried in time the more glaring are the colors in which their deeds are painted, and with a loud cry of woe our village eventually hears how an Empress drank her husband's blood in long draughts thousands of years ago.

Thus, then, do our people deal with departed emperors, but the living ruler they confuse among the dead. If once, only once in a man's lifetime, an imperial official on his tour of the provinces should arrive by chance at our village, make certain announcements in the name of the government, scrutinize the tax lists, examine the school children, inquire of the priest regarding our doings and affairs, and then, before he steps into his sedan chair, should sum up his impressions in verbose admonitions to the assembled commune—then a smile flits over every face, people throw surreptitious glances at each other, and bend over their children so as not to be observed by the official. Why, they think to themselves, he's speaking of a dead man as if he were alive, this Emperor of his died long ago, the dynasty is blotted out, the good official is having his joke with us, but we will behave as if we did not notice it, so as not to offend him. But we shall obey in earnest no one but our present ruler, for not to do so would be a crime. And behind the departing sedan chair of the official there rises in might as ruler of the village some figure fortuitously exalted from an urn already crumbled to dust.

Similarly our people are but little affected by revolutions in the state or contemporary wars. I recall an incident in my youth. A revolt had broken out in a neighboring, but yet quite distant, province. What caused it I can no longer remember, nor is it of any importance now; occasions for revolt can be found there any day, the people are an excitable people. Well, one day a leaflet published by the rebels was brought to my father's house by a beggar who had crossed that province. It happened to be a feast day, our rooms were filled with guests, the priest sat in the center and studied the sheet. Suddenly everybody started to laugh, in the confusion the sheet was torn, the beggar, who however had already received abundant alms, was driven out of the room with blows, the guests dispersed to enjoy the beautiful day. Why?

The dialect of this neighboring province differs in some essential respects from ours, and this difference occurs also in certain turns of the written word, which for us have an archaic character. Hardly had the priest read two pages before we had come to our decision. Ancient history told long ago, old sorrows long since healed. And though—so it seems to to me in recollection—the gruesomeness of the living present was irrefutably conveyed by the beggar's words, we laughed and shook our heads and refused to listen any longer. So eager are our people to obliterate the present.

If from such appearances anyone should draw the conclusion that in reality we have no Emperor, he would not be far from the truth. Over and over again it must be repeated: There is perhaps no people more faithful to the Emperor than ours in the south, but the Emperor derives no advantage from our fidelity. True, the sacred dragon stands on the little column at the end of our village, and ever since the beginning of human memory it has breathed out its fiery breath in the direction of Peking in token of homage—but Peking itself is far stranger to the people in our village than the next world. Can there really be a village where the houses stand side by side, covering all the fields for a greater distance than one can see from our hills, and can there be dense crowds of people packed between these houses day and night? We find it more difficult to picture such a city than to believe that Peking and its Emperor are one, a cloud, say, peacefully voyaging beneath the sun in the course of the ages.

Now the result of holding such opinions is a life on the whole free and unconstrained. By no means immoral, however; hardly ever have I found in my travels such pure morals as in my native village. But yet a life that is subject to no contemporary law, and attends only to the exhortations and warnings which come to us from olden times.

I guard against generalizations, and do not assert that in all the ten thousand villages in my province it is so, far less

The Great Wall of China 97

in all the five hundred provinces of China. Yet perhaps I may venture to assert on the basis of the many writings on this subject which I have read, as well as from my own observation—the building of the wall in particular, with its abundance of human material, provided a man of sensibility with the opportunity of traversing the souls of almost all the provinces—on the basis of all this, then, perhaps I may venture to assert that the prevailing attitude to the Emperor shows persistently and universally something fundamentally in common with that of our village. Now I have no wish whatever to represent this attitude as a virtue; on the contrary. True, the essential responsibility for it lies with the government, which in the most ancient empire in the world has not yet succeeded in developing, or has neglected to develop, the institution of the empire to such precision that its workings extend directly and unceasingly to the farthest frontiers of the land. On the other hand, however, there is also involved a certain feebleness of faith and imaginative power on the part of the people, that prevents them from raising the empire out of its stagnation in Peking and clasping it in all its palpable living reality to their own breasts, which yet desire nothing better than but once to feel that touch and then to die.

This attitude then is certainly no virtue. All the more remarkable is it that this very weakness should seem to be one of the greatest unifying influences among our people; indeed, if one may dare to use the expression, the very ground on which we live. To set about establishing a fundamental defect here would mean undermining not only our consciences, but, what is far worse, our feet. And for that reason I shall not proceed any further at this stage with my inquiry into these questions.

THE VILLAGE SCHOOLMASTER
[THE GIANT MOLE]

THOSE, and I am one of them, who find even a small ordinary sized mole disgusting, would probably have died of disgust if they had seen the giant mole that a few years back was observed in the neighborhood of one of our villages, which achieved a certain transitory celebrity on account of the incident. Today it has long since sunk back into oblivion again, and in that only shares the obscurity of the whole incident, which has remained quite inexplicable, but which people, it must be confessed, have also taken no great pains to explain; and as a result of an incomprehensible apathy in those very circles which should have concerned themselves with it, and who in fact have shown enthusiastic interest in far more trifling matters, the affair has been forgotten without ever being adequately investigated. In any case, the fact that the village could not be reached by the railroad was no excuse. Many people came from great distances out of pure curiosity, there were even foreigners among them; it was only those who should have shown something more than curiosity that refrained from coming. In fact, if a few quite simple people, people whose daily work gave them hardly a moment of leisure—if these people had not quite disinterestedly taken up the affair, the rumor of this natural phenomenon would probably have never spread beyond the locality. Indeed, rumor itself, which usually cannot be held within bounds, was actually sluggish in this case; if it had not literally been given a shove it would not have spread. But even that was no valid reason for refusing to inquire into the affair; on the contrary this second phenomenon should have been investigated as well. Instead the old village schoolmaster was left to write the sole account in black and white of the incident, and though he was an excellent man in his own profession, neither his abilities nor his equipment made it possible for him to produce an exhaustive description that could be used as a foundation by others, far less, therefore, an actual explanation of the occurrence. His little pamphlet was printed, and a good many copies were sold to visitors to the village about that time; it also received some public recognition, but the teacher was wise enough to perceive that his fragmentary labors, in which no one supported him, were basically without value. If in spite of that he did not relax in them, and made the question his lifework, though it naturally became more hopeless from year to year, that only shows on the one hand how powerful an effect the appearance of the giant mole was capable of producing, and on the other how much laborious effort and fidelity to his convictions may be found in an old and obscure village schoolmaster. But that he suffered deeply from the cold attitude of the recognized authorities is proved by a brief brochure with which he followed up his pamphlet several years later, by which time hardly anyone could remember what it was all about. In this brochure he complained of the lack of understanding that he had encountered in people where it was least to be expected; complaints which carried conviction less by the skill with which they were expressed than by their honesty. Of such people he said very appositely: "It is not I, but they, who talk like old village schoolmasters." And among other things he adduced the pro-

nouncement of a scholar to whom he had gone expressly
about his affair. The name of the scholar was not mentioned,
but from various circumstances we could guess who it was.
After the teacher had managed with great difficulty to secure
admittance, he perceived at once from the very way in which
he was greeted that the savant had already acquired a rooted
prejudice against the matter. The absent-mindedness with
which he listened to the long report which the teacher,
pamphlet in hand, delivered to him, can be gauged from a
remark that he let fall after a pause for ostensible reflection:
"The soil in your neighborhood is particularly black and rich.
Consequently it provides the moles with particularly rich
nourishment, and so they grow to an unusual size."

"But not to such a size as that!" exclaimed the teacher,
and he measured off two yards on the wall, somewhat ex-
aggerating the length of the mole in his exasperation. "Oh,
and why not?" replied the scholar, who obviously looked
upon the whole affair as a great joke. With this verdict the
teacher had to return to his home. He tells how his wife and
six children were waiting for him by the roadside in the snow,
and how he had to admit to them the final collapse of his
hopes.

When I read of the scholar's attitude towards the old man
I was not yet acquainted with the teacher's pamphlet. But I
at once resolved myself to collect and correlate all the information I could discover regarding the case. If I could not
employ physical force against the scholar, I could at least
write a defense of the teacher, or more exactly, of the good
intentions of an honest but uninfluential man. I admit that
I rued this decision later, for I soon saw that its execution
was bound to involve me in a very strange predicament. On
the one hand my own influence was far from sufficient to
effect a change in learned or even public opinion in the
teacher's favor, while on the other the teacher was bound
to notice that I was less concerned with his main object,

which was to prove that the giant mole had actually been seen, than to defend his honesty, which must naturally be self-evident to him and in need of no defense. Accordingly, what was bound to happen was this: I would be misunderstood by the teacher, though I wanted to collaborate with him, and instead of helping him I myself would probably require support, which was most unlikely to appear. Besides, my decision would impose a great burden of work upon me. If I wanted to convince people I could not invoke the teacher, since he himself had not been able to convince them. To read his pamphlet could only have led me astray, and so I refrained from reading it until I should have finished my own labors. More, I did not even get in touch with the teacher. True, he heard of my inquiries through intermediaries, but he did not know whether I was working for him or against him. In fact he probably assumed the latter, though he denied it later on; for I have proof of the fact that he put various obstacles in my way. It was quite easy for him to do that, for of course I was compelled to undertake anew all the inquiries he had already made, and so he could always steal a march on me. But that was the only objection that could be justly made to my method, an unavoidable reproach, but one which was palliated by the caution and self-abnegation with which I drew my conclusions. But for the rest my pamphlet was quite uninfluenced by the teacher, perhaps on this point, indeed, I showed all too great a scrupulosity; from my words one might have thought nobody had ever inquired into the case before, and I was the first to interrogate those who had seen or heard of the mole, the first to correlate the evidence, the first to draw conclusions. When later I read the schoolmaster's pamphlet—it had a very circumstantial title: "A mole, larger in size than ever seen before"—I found that we actually did not agree on certain important points, though we both believed we had proved our main point, namely, the existence of the mole. These differences prevented the establishment of the friendly relations with the schoolmaster that I had been looking forward to in spite of everything. On his side there developed a feeling almost of hostility. True, he was always modest and humble in his bearing towards me, but that only made his real feelings the more obvious. In other words, he was of the opinion that I had merely damaged his credit, and that my belief that I had been or could be of assistance to him was simplicity at best, but more likely presumption or artifice. He was particularly fond of saying that all his previous enemies had shown their hostility either not at all, or in private, or at most by word of mouth, while I had considered it necessary to have my censures straightway published. Moreover, the few opponents of his who had really occupied themselves with the subject, if but superficially, had at least listened to his, the schoolmaster's, views before they had given expression to their own: while I, on the strength of unsystematically assembled and in part misunderstood evidence, had published conclusions which, even if they were correct as regarded the main point, must evoke incredulity, and among the public no less than the educated. But the faintest hint that the existence of the mole was unworthy of credence was the worst thing that could happen in this case.

To these reproaches, veiled as they were, I could easily have found an answer—for instance, that his own pamphlet achieved the very summit of the incredible—it was less easy, however, to make headway against his continual suspicion, and that was the reason why I was very reserved in my dealings with him. For in his heart he was convinced that I wanted to rob him of the fame of being the first man publicly to vindicate the mole. Now of course he really enjoyed no fame whatever, but only an absurd notoriety that was shrinking more and more, and for which I had certainly no desire to compete. Besides, in the foreword to my pamphlet I had expressly declared that the teacher must stand for all

time as the discoverer of the mole—and he was not even that
—and that only my sympathy with his unfortunate fate had
spurred me on to write. "It is the aim of this pamphlet"—
so I ended up all too melodramtically, but it corresponded
with my feelings at that time—"to help in giving the schoolmaster's book the wide publicity it deserves. If I succeed in
that, then may my name, which I regard as only tran-
siently and indirectly associated with this question, be blotted
from it at once." Thus I disclaimed expressly any major
participation in the affair; it was almost as if I had foreseen
in some manner the teacher's unbelievable reproaches. Nevertheless he found in that very passage a handle against me,
and I do not deny that there was a faint show of justice in
what he said or rather hinted; indeed I was often struck by
the fact that he showed almost a keener penetration where
I was concerned than he had done in his pamphlet. For he
maintained that my foreword was double-faced. If I was
really concerned solely to give publicity to his pamphlet, why
had I not occupied myself exclusively with him and his
pamphlet, why had I not pointed out its virtues, its irrefuta-
bility, why had I not confined myself to insisting on the
significance of the discovery and making that clear, why had
I instead tackled the discovery itself, while completely ignoring the pamphlet? Had not the discovery been made already?
Was there still anything left to be done in that direction?
But if I really thought that it was necessary for me to make
the discovery all over again, why had I disassociated myself
from the discovery so solemnly in my foreword? One might
put that down to false modesty, but it was something worse.
I was trying to belittle the discovery, I was drawing attention
to it merely for the purpose of depreciating it, while he on
the other hand had inquired into and finally established it.
Perhaps the affair had sunk somewhat into desuetude; now
I had made a noise about it again, but at the same time I
had made the schoolmaster's position more difficult than ever.

What did he care whether his honesty was vindicated or not? All that he was concerned with was the thing itself, and with that alone. But I was only of disservice to it, for I did not understand it, I did not prize it at its true value, I had no real feeling for it. It was infinitely above my intellectual capacity. He sat before me and looked at me, his old wrinkled face quite composed, and yet this was what he was thinking. Yet it was not true that he was only concerned with the thing itself: actually he was very greedy for fame, and wanted to make money out of the business too, which, however, considering his large family, was very understandable. Nevertheless my interest in the affair seemed so trivial compared with his own, that he felt he could claim to be completely disinterested without deviating very seriously from the truth. And indeed my inner doubts refused to be quite calmed by my telling myself that the man's reproaches were really due to the fact that he clung to his mole, so to speak, with both hands, and was bound to look upon anyone who laid even a finger on it as a traitor. For that was not true; his attitude was not to be explained by greed, or at any rate by greed alone, but rather by the touchiness which his great labors and their complete unsuccess had bred in him. Yet even his touchiness did not explain everything. Perhaps my interest in the affair was really too trivial. The schoolmaster was used to lack of interest in strangers. He regarded it as a universal evil, but no longer suffered from its individual manifestations. Now a man had appeared who, strangely enough, took up the affair; and even he did not understand it. Attacked from this side I can make no defense. I am no zoologist; yet perhaps I would have thrown myself into the case with my whole heart if I had discovered it; but I had not discovered it. Such a gigantic mole is certainly a prodigy, yet one cannot expect the continuous and undivided attention of the whole world to be accorded it, particularly if its existence is not completely and irrefutably established, and in any case it cannot be produced.

And I admit too that even if I had been the discoverer I would probably never have come forward so gladly and voluntarily in defense of the mole as I had in that of the schoolmaster.

Now the misunderstanding between me and the schoolmaster would probably have quickly cleared up if my pamphlet had achieved success. But success was not forthcoming. Perhaps the book was not well enough written, not persuasive enough; I am a businessman, it may be that the composition of such a pamphlet was still further beyond my limited powers than those of the teacher, though in the kind of knowledge required I was greatly superior to him. Besides, my unsuccess may be explicable in other ways; the time at which the pamphlet appeared may have been inauspicious. The discovery of the mole, which had failed to penetrate to a wide public at the time it took place, was not so long past on the one hand as to be completely forgotten, and thus capable of being brought alive again by my pamphlet, while on the other hand enough time had elapsed quite to exhaust the trivial interest that had originally existed. Those who took my pamphlet at all seriously told themselves, in that bored tone which from the first had characterized the debate, that now the old useless labors on this wearisome question were to begin all over again; and some even confused my pamphlet with the schoolmaster's. In a leading agricultural journal appeared the following comment, fortunately at the very end, and in small print: "The pamphlet on the giant mole has once more been sent to us. Years ago we remember having had a hearty laugh over it. Since then it has not become more intelligible, nor we more hard of understanding. But we simply refuse to laugh at it a second time. Instead, we would ask our teaching associations whether more useful work cannot be found for our village schoolmasters than hunting out giant moles." An unpardonable confusion of identity. They had read neither the first nor the second pamphlet, and the two perfunctorily scanned expressions, "giant mole" and "village schoolmaster," were sufficient for these gentlemen, as representatives of publicly esteemed interest, to pronounce on the subject. Against this attack measures might have been attempted and with success, but the lack of understanding between the teacher and myself kept me from venturing upon them. I tried instead to keep the review from his knowledge as long as I could. But he very soon discovered it, as I recognized from a sentence in one of his letters, in which he announced his intention of visiting me for the Christmas holidays. He wrote: "The world is full of malice, and people smooth the path for it," by which he wished to convey that I was one of the malicious, but, not content with my own innate malice, wished also to make the world's path smooth for it: in other words, was acting in such a way as to arouse the general malice and help it to victory. Well, I summoned the resolution I required, and was able to await him calmly, and calmly greet him when he arrived, this time a shade less polite in his bearing than usual; he carefully drew out the journal from the breast pocket of his old-fashioned padded overcoat, and opening it handed it to me. "I've seen it," I replied, handing the journal back unread. "You've seen it," he said with a sigh; he had the old teacher's habit of repeating the other person's answers. "Of course I won't take this lying down!" he went on, tapping the journal excitedly with his finger and glancing up sharply at me, as if I were of a different mind; he certainly had some idea of what I was about to say, for I think I have noticed, not so much from his words as from other indications, that he often has a genuine intuition of my intentions, though he never yields to them but lets himself be diverted. What I said to him I can set down almost word for word, for I made a note of it shortly after our interview. "Do what you like," I said, "our ways part from this moment. I fancy that that is neither unexpected nor unwelcome news to you. The review in this journal is not the real reason for my decision; it has merely finally confirmed it. The real reason is this: originally I thought my intervention might be of some use to you, while now I cannot but recog-

nize that I have damaged you in every direction. Why it has
turned out so I cannot say; the causes of success and unsuccess
are always ambiguous; but don't look for the sole explanation
in my shortcomings. Consider: you too had the best intentions,
and yet, if one regards the matter objectively, you failed. I
don't intend it as a joke, for it would be a joke against myself,
when I say that your connection with me must unfortunately
be counted among your failures. It is neither cowardice nor
treachery, if I withdraw from the affair now. Actually it involves a certain degree of self-renunciation; my pamphlet itself proves how much I respect you personally, in a certain
sense you have become my teacher, and I have almost grown
fond of the mole itself. Nevertheless I have decided to step
aside; you are the discoverer, and all that I can do is to prevent
you from gaining possible fame, while I attract failure and pass
it on to you. At least that is your own opinion. Enough of that.
The sole expiation that I can make is to beg your forgiveness
and, should you require it, to publish openly, that is, in this
journal, the admission I have just made to you."

These were my words; they were not entirely sincere, but
what was sincere in them was obvious enough. My explanation had the effect upon him that I had roughly anticipated.
Most old people have something deceitful, something menda-
cious, in their dealings with people younger than themselves;
you live at peace with them, imagine you are on the best of
terms with them, know their ruling prejudices, receive continual assurances of amity, take the whole thing for granted; and
when something decisive happens and those peaceful relations,
so long nourished, should come into effective operation, suddenly these old people rise before you like strangers, show that
they have deeper and stronger convictions, and now for the
first time literally unfurl their banner, and with terror you read
upon it the new decree. The reason for this terror lies chiefly
in the fact that what the old say now is really far more just and
sensible than what they had said before; it is as if even the self-

evident had degrees of validity, and their words now were more self-evident than ever. But the final deceit that lies in their words consists in this, that at bottom they have always said what they are saying now. I must have probed deeply into the schoolmaster, seeing that his next words did not entirely take me by surprise. "Child," he said, laying his hand on mine and patting it gently, "how did you ever take it into your head to go into this affair? The very first I heard of it I talked it over with my wife." He pushed his chair back from the table, got up, spread out his arms, and stared at the floor, as if his tiny little wife were standing there and he were speaking to her. " 'We've struggled on alone,' I said to her, 'for many years; now, it seems, a noble protector has risen for us in the city, a fine businessman, Mr. So-and-so. We should congratulate ourselves, shouldn't we? A businessman in the city isn't to be sniffed at; when an ignorant peasant believes us and says so it doesn't help us, for what a peasant may say or do is of no account; whether he says the old village schoolmaster is right, or spits to show his contempt, the net result is the same. And if instead of one peasant ten thousand should stand up for us, the result, if possible, would only be still worse. A businessman in the city, on the other hand, that's something else again; a man like that has connections, things he says in passing, as it were, are taken up and repeated, new patrons interest themselves in the question, one of them, it may be, remarks: You can learn even from old village schoolmasters, and next day whole crowds of people are saying it to one another, people you would never imagine saying such things, to look at them. Next, money is found to finance the business, one gentleman goes around collecting for it and the others shower subscriptions on him; they decide that the village schoolmaster must be dragged from his obscurity; they arrive, they don't bother about his external appearance, but take him to their bosoms, and since his wife and children hang on to him, they are taken along too. Have you ever watched city people? They chatter without stopping. When there's a whole lot of them together you can hear their chatter running from right to left and back again, and up and down, this way and that. And so, chattering away, they push us into the coach, so that we've hardly time to bow to everybody. The gentleman on the coachman's seat puts his glasses straight, flourishes his whip, and off we go. They all wave a parting greeting to the village, as if we were still there and not sitting among them. The more impatient city people drive out in carriages to meet us. As we approach they get up from their seats and crane their necks. The gentleman who collected the money arranges everything methodically and in order. When we drive into the city we are a long procession of carriages. We think the public welcome is over; but it really only begins when we reach our hotel. In a city an announcement attracts a great many people. What interests one interests all the rest immediatcly. They take their views from one another and promptly make those views their own. All the people who haven't managed to drive out and meet us in carriages are waiting in front of the hotel; others could have driven out, but they were too self-conscious. They're waiting too. It's extraordinary, the way that the gentleman who collected the money keeps his eye on everything and directs everything.' "

I had listened coolly to him, indeed I had grown cooler and cooler while he went on. On the table I had piled up all the copies of my pamphlet in my possession. Only a few were missing, for during the past week I had sent out a circular demanding the return of all the copies distributed, and had received most of them back. True, from several quarters I had got very polite notes saying that So-and-so could not remember having received such a pamphlet, and that, if it had actually arrived, he was sorry to confess that he must have lost it. Even that was gratifying; in my heart I desired nothing better. Only one reader begged me to let him keep the pamphlet as a curiosity, pledging himself, in accordance with the spirit of my circular, to show it to no one for twenty years. The village teacher had not yet seen my circular. I was glad that his words made it so easy for me to show it to him. I could do that without anxiety in any case, however, as I had drawn it up very circumspectly, keeping his interests in mind the whole time. The crucial passage in the circular ran as follows: "I do not ask for the return of the pamphlet because I retract in any way the opinions defended there or wish them to be regarded as erroneous or even undemonstrable on any point. My request has purely personal and moreover very urgent grounds; but no conclusion whatever must be drawn from it as regards my attitude to the whole matter. I beg to draw your particular attention to this, and would be glad also if you would make the fact better known."

For the time being I kept my hand over the circular and said: "You reproach me in your heart because things have not turned out as you hoped. Why do that? Don't let us embitter our last moments together. And do try to see that, though you've made a discovery, it isn't necessarily greater than every other discovery, and consequently the injustice you suffer under any greater than other injustices. I don't know the ways of learned societies, but I can't believe that in the most favorable circumstances you would have been given a reception even remotely resembling the one you seem to have described to your wife. While I myself still hoped that something might come of my pamphlet, the most I expected was that perhaps the attention of a professor might be drawn to our case, that he might commission some young student to inquire into it, that this student might visit you and check in his own fashion your and my inquiries once more on the spot, and that finally, if the results seemed to him worth consideration—we must not forget that all young students are full of skepticism—he might bring out a pamphlet of his own in which your discoveries would be put on a scientific basis. All the same, even if that hope had been realized nothing very much would have been

achieved. The student's pamphlet, supporting such queer opinions, would probably be held up to ridicule. If you take this
agricultural journal as a sample, you can see how easily that
may happen; and scientific periodicals are still more ruthless
in such matters. And that's quite understandable; professors
bear a great responsibility towards themselves, towards science,
towards posterity; they can't take every new discovery to their
bosoms straight away. We others have the advantage of them
there. But I'll leave that out of account and assume that the
student's pamphlet has found acceptance. What would happen next? You would probably receive honorable mention, and
that might perhaps benefit your profession too; people would
say: 'Our village schoolmasters have sharp eyes'; and this
journal, if journals have a memory or a conscience, would be
forced to make you a public apology; also some well-inten-
tioned professor would be found to secure a scholarship for
you; it's possible they might even get you to come to the city,
find a post for you in some school, and so give you a chance
of using the scientific resources of a city so as to improve yourself. But if I am to be quite frank, I think they would content themselves with merely trying to do all this. They would
summon you and you would appear, but only as an ordinary
petitioner like hundreds of others, and not in solemn state;
they would talk to you and praise your honest efforts, but they
would see at the same time that you were an old man, that it
was hopeless for anyone to begin to study science at such an
age, and moreover that you had hit upon your discovery more
by chance than by design, and had besides no ambition to extend your labors beyond this one case. For these reasons they
would probably send you back to your village again. Your
discovery, of course, would be carried further, for it is not so
trifling that, once having achieved recognition, it could be
forgotten again. But you would not hear much more about it,
and what you heard you would scarcely understand. Every
new discovery is assumed at once into the sum total of knowl-

edge, and with that ceases in a sense to be a discovery; it dissolves into the whole and disappears, and one must have a trained scientific eye even to recognize it after that. For it is related to fundamental axioms of whose existence we don't even know, and in the debates of science it is raised on these axioms into the very clouds. How can we expect to understand such things? Often as we listen to some learned discussion we may be under the impression that it is about your discovery, when it is about something quite different, and the next time, when we think it is about something else, and not about your discovery at all, it may turn out to be about that and that alone.

"Don't you see that? You would remain in your village, you would be able with the extra money to feed and clothe your family a little better; but your discovery would be taken out of your hands, and without your being able with any show of justice to object; for only in the city could it be given its final seal. And people wouldn't be altogether ungrateful to you, they might build a little museum on the spot where the discovery was made, it would become one of the sights of the village, you would be given the keys to keep, and, so that you shouldn't lack some outward token of honor, they could give you a little medal to wear on the breast of your coat, like those worn by attendants in scientific institutions. All this might have been possible; but was it what you wanted?"

Without stopping to consider his answer he turned on me and said: "And so that's what you wanted to achieve for me?"

"Probably," I said, "I didn't consider what I was doing carefully enough at the time to be able to answer that clearly now. I wanted to help you, but that was a failure, and the worst failure I have ever had. That's why I want to withdraw now and undo what I've done as far as I'm able."

"Well and good," said the teacher, taking out his pipe and beginning to fill it with the tobacco that he carried loose in all his pockets. "You took up this thankless business of your own free will, and now of your own free will you withdraw. So that's all right."

"I'm not an obstinate man," I said. "Do you find anything to object to in my proposal?"

"No, absolutely nothing," said the schoolmaster, and his pipe was already going. I could not bear the stink of his tobacco, and so I rose and began to walk up and down the room. From previous encounters I was used to the teacher's extreme taciturnity, and to the fact that in spite of it he never seemed to have any desire to stir from my room once he was in it. That had often disturbed me before. He wants something more, I always thought at such times, and I would offer him money, which indeed he invariably accepted. Yet he never went away before it suited his convenience. Generally his pipe was smoked out by that time, then he would ceremoniously and respectfully push his chair in to the table, make a detour around it, seize his cane standing in the corner, press my hand warmly, and go. But today his silent presence as he sat there was an actual torture to me. When one has bidden a last farewell to someone, as I had done, a farewell accepted in good faith, surely the mutual formalities that remain should be got over as quickly as possible, and one should not burden one's host purposelessly with one's silent presence. As I contemplated the stubborn little old fellow from behind, while he sat at the table, it seemed an impossible idea ever to show him the door.

THE HUNTER GRACCHUS

TWO BOYS were sitting on the harbor wall playing with dice. A man was reading a newspaper on the steps of the monument, resting in the shadow of a hero who was flourishing his sword on high. A girl was filling her bucket at the fountain. A fruitseller was lying beside his wares, gazing at the lake. Through the vacant window and door openings of a café one could see two men quite at the back drinking their wine. The proprietor was sitting at a table in front and dozing. A bark was silently making for the little harbor, as if borne by invisible means over the water. A man in a blue blouse climbed ashore and drew the rope through a ring. Behind the boatman two other men in dark coats with silver buttons carried a bier, on which, beneath a great flower-patterned fringed silk cloth, a man was apparently lying.

Nobody on the quay troubled about the newcomers; even when they lowered the bier to wait for the boatman, who was still occupied with his rope, nobody went nearer, nobody asked them a question, nobody accorded them an inquisitive glance.

The pilot was still further detained by a woman who, a child at her breast, now appeared with loosened hair on the deck of the boat. Then he advanced and indicated a yellowish two-storeyed house that rose abruptly on the left near the water; the bearers took up their burden and bore it to the low but gracefully pillared door. A little boy opened a window just in time to see the party vanishing into the house, then hastily shut the window again. The door too was now shut; it was of black oak, and very strongly made. A flock of doves which had been flying around the belfry alighted in the street before the house. As if their food were stored within, they assembled in front of the door. One of them flew up to the first storey and pecked at the windowpane. They were bright-hued, well- tended, lively birds. The woman on the boat flung grain to them in a wide sweep; they ate it up and flew across to the woman.

A man in a top hat tied with a band of black crêpe now descended one of the narrow and very steep lanes that led to the harbor. He glanced around vigilantly, everything seemed to distress him, his mouth twisted at the sight of some offal in a corner. Fruit skins were lying on the steps of the monument; he swept them off in passing with his stick. He rapped at the house door, at the same time taking his top hat from his head with his black-gloved hand. The door was opened at once, and some fifty little boys appeared in two rows in the long entry-hall, and bowed to him.

The boatman descended the stairs, greeted the gentleman in black, conducted him up to the first storey, led him around the bright and elegant loggia which encircled the courtyard, and both of them entered, while the boys pressed after them at a respectful distance, a cool spacious room looking towards the back, from whose window no habitation, but only a bare, blackish grey rocky wall was to be seen. The bearers were busied in setting up and lighting several long candles at the head of the bier, yet these did not give light, but only disturbed the shadows which had been immobile till then, and made them flicker over the walls. The cloth covering the bier had been thrown back. Lying on it was a man with wildly matted hair, who looked somewhat like a hunter. He lay without motion and, it seemed, without breathing, his eyes closed; yet only his trappings indicated that this man was probably dead.

The gentleman stepped up to the bier, laid his hand on the brow of the man lying upon it, then kneeled down and prayed. The boatman made a sign to the bearers to leave the room; they went out, drove away the boys who had gathered outside, and shut the door. But even that did not seem to satisfy the gentleman, he glanced at the boatman; the boatman understood, and vanished through a side door into the next room. At once the man on the bier opened his eyes, turned his face painfully towards the gentleman, and said: "Who are you?" Without any mark of surprise the gentleman rose from his kneeling posture and answered: "The Burgomaster of Riva."

The man on the bier nodded, indicated a chair with a feeble movement of his arm, and said, after the Burgomaster had accepted his invitation: "I knew that, of course, Burgomaster, but in the first moments of returning consciousness I always forget, everything goes around before my eyes, and it is best to ask about anything even if I know. You too probably know that I am the hunter Gracchus."

"Certainly," said the Burgomaster. "Your arrival was announced to me during the night. We had been asleep for a good while. Then towards midnight my wife cried: 'Salvatore'—that's my name—'look at that dove at the window.' It was really a dove, but as big as a cock. It flew over me and said in my ear: 'Tomorrow the dead hunter Gracchus is coming; receive him in the name of the city.'"

The hunter nodded and licked his lips with the tip of his tongue: "Yes, the doves flew here before me. But do you believe, Burgomaster, that I shall remain in Riva?"

"I cannot say that yet," replied the Burgomaster. "Are you dead?"

"Yes," said the hunter, "as you see. Many years ago, yes, it must be a great many years ago, I fell from a precipice in the

Black Forest—that is in Germany—when I was hunting a chamois. Since then I have been dead."

"But you are alive too," said the Burgomaster.

"In a certain sense," said the hunter, "in a certain sense I am alive too. My death ship lost its way; a wrong turn of the wheel, a moment's absence of mind on the pilot's part, the distraction of my lovely native country, I cannot tell what it was; I only know this, that I remained on earth and that ever since my ship has sailed earthly waters. So I, who asked for nothing better than to live among my mountains, travel after my death through all the lands of the earth."

"And you have no part in the other world?" asked the Burgomaster, knitting his brow.

"I am forever," replied the hunter, "on the great stair that leads up to it. On that infinitely wide and spacious stair I clamber about, sometimes up, sometimes down, sometimes on the right, sometimes on the left, always in motion. The hunter has been turned into a butterfly. Do not laugh."

"I am not laughing," said the Burgomaster in self-defense.

"That is very good of you," said the hunter. "I am always in motion. But when I make a supreme flight and see the gate actually shining before me I awaken presently on my old ship, still stranded forlornly in some earthly sea or other. The fundamental error of my one-time death grins at me as I lie in my cabin. Julia, the wife of the pilot, knocks at the door and brings me on my bier the morning drink of the land whose coasts we chance to be passing. I lie on a wooden pallet, I wear—it cannot be a pleasure to look at me—a filthy winding sheet, my hair and beard, black tinged with grey, have grown together inextricably, my limbs are covered with a great flower-patterned woman's shawl with long fringes. A sacramental candle stands at my head and lights me. On the wall opposite me is a little picture, evidently of a bushman who is aiming his spear at me and taking cover as best he can behind a beautifully painted shield. On shipboard one often comes across silly pictures, but that is the silliest of them all. Otherwise my wooden cage is quite empty. Through a hole in the side the warm airs of the southern night come in, and I hear the water slapping against the old boat.

"I have lain here ever since the time when, as the hunter Gracchus living in the Black Forest, I followed a chamois and fell from a precipice. Everything happened in good order. I pursued, I fell, bled to death in a ravine, died, and this ship should have conveyed me to the next world. I can still remember how gladly I stretched myself out on this pallet for the first time. Never did the mountains listen to such songs from me as these shadowy walls did then.

"I had been glad to live and I was glad to die. Before I stepped aboard, I joyfully flung away my wretched load of ammunition, my knapsack, my hunting rifle that I had always been proud to carry, and I slipped into my winding sheet like a girl into her marriage dress. I lay and waited. Then came the mishap."

"A terrible fate," said the Burgomaster, raising his hand defensively. "And you bear no blame for it?"

"None," said the hunter. "I was a hunter; was there any sin in that? I followed my calling as a hunter in the Black Forest, where there were still wolves in those days. I lay in ambush, shot, hit my mark, flayed the skins from my victims: was there any sin in that? My labors were blessed. 'The great hunter of the Black Forest' was the name I was given. Was there any sin in that?"

"I am not called upon to decide that," said the Burgomaster, "but to me also there seems to be no sin in such things. But then, whose is the guilt?"

"The boatman's," said the hunter. "Nobody will read what I say here, no one will come to help me; even if all the people were commanded to help me, every door and window would remain shut, everybody would take to bed and draw the bedclothes over his head, the whole earth would become an inn for the night. And there is sense in that, for nobody knows of me, and if anyone knew he would not know where I could be found, and if he knew where I could be found, he would not know how to deal with me, he would not know how to help me. The thought of helping me is an illness that has to be cured by taking to one's bed.

"I know that, and so I do not shout to summon help, even though at moments—when I lose control over myself, as I have done just now, for instance—I think seriously of it. But to drive out such thoughts I need only look around me and verify where I am, and—I can safely assert—have been for hundreds of years."

"Extraordinary," said the Burgomaster, "extraordinary. And now do you think of staying here in Riva with us?"

"I think not," said the hunter with a smile, and, to excuse himself, he laid his hand on the Burgomaster's knee. "I am here, more than that I do not know, further than that I cannot go. My ship has no rudder, and it is driven by the wind that blows in the undermost regions of death."

THE MARRIED COUPLE

BUSINESS IN GENERAL is so bad that sometimes, when my work
in the office leaves me a little time, I myself pick up the case
of samples and call on my customers personally. Long since I
had intended to visit some time, among others, N., with whom
once I had constant business relations, which, however, during
the last year have almost completely lapsed for some reason
unknown to me. Besides, there need not always be real reasons
for such disruptions; in the present unstable state of affairs
often a mere nothing, a mood, will turn the scale, and in the
same way a mere nothing, a word, can put things right again.
To gain admittance to N., however, is a somewhat ticklish
business; he is an old man, grown somewhat infirm too of late,
and though he still insists on attending to business matters
himself, he is hardly ever to be seen in his office; if you want
to speak to him you have to go to his house, and one likes to
put off a business call of that kind.

Last evening after six I nevertheless set out for his house; it
was really no time for paying calls, but my visit after all was a
business, not a social, one, and might be regarded accordingly.
I was in luck. N. was in; he had just come back with his wife
from a walk, the servant told me, and was now in the bedroom
of his son, who was unwell and confined to his bed. I was re-

quested to go there; at first I hesitated, but then the desire to get my disagreeable visit over as quickly as possible turned the scale, and I allowed myself to be conducted as I was, in my overcoat and hat with my case of samples, through a dark room into a faintly lit one, where a small company was gathered.

My first glance fell, probably by instinct, on an agent only too well known to me, a trade rival of myself in some respects. So he had stolen a march on me, it seemed. He was sitting comfortably by the bed of the sick man, just as if he were a doctor; he sat brazenly there in his beautiful ample overcoat, which was unbuttoned; the sick man too probably had his own thoughts as he lay there with his cheeks faintly flushed with fever, now and then glancing at his visitor. He was no longer young either, N.'s son, a man of about my own age with a short beard, somewhat unkempt on account of his illness. Old N., a tall, broad-shouldered man, but to my astonishment grown very thin because of some creeping malady, bent and infirm, was still wearing the fur coat in which he had entered, and mumbling something to his son. His wife, small and frail, but immensely vivacious, yet only when she spoke to him—us others she scarcely noticed—was occupied in helping him to take off his overcoat, which, considering the great difference in their height, was a matter of some difficulty, but at last was achieved. Perhaps, indeed, the real difficulty was caused by N.'s impatience, for with restless hands he kept on feeling for the easy chair, which his wife, after the overcoat was off, quickly pushed forward for him. She herself then took up the fur coat, beneath which she almost vanished, and carried it out.

Now at last, it seemed to me, my moment had come, or rather it had not come and probably would never come; yet if I was to attempt anything it must be done at once, for I felt that here the conditions for a business interview could only become increasingly unfavorable; and to plant myself down here for all time, as the agent apparently intended, was not my way: besides, I did not want to take the slightest notice of him. So I began without ceremony to state my business, although I saw that N. would have liked at that moment to have a chat with his son. Unfortunately I have a habit when I have worked myself up—and that takes a very short time, and on this occasion took a shorter time than usual—of getting up and walking about while I am talking. Though a very good arrangement in one's own office, in a strange house it may be somewhat burdensome. But I could not restrain myself, particularly as I was feeling the lack of my usual cigarette. Well, every man has his bad habits, yet I can congratulate myself on mine when I think of the agent's. For what is to be said of his behavior, of the fact, for instance, that every now and then he would suddenly and quite unexpectedly clap his hat on his head; he had been holding it on his knee until then, slowly pushing it up and down there. True, he took it off again immediately, as if he had made a blunder, but he had had it on his head nevertheless for a second or two, and besides he repeated this performance again and again every few minutes. Surely such conduct must be called unpardonable. It did not disturb me, however, I walked up and down, completely absorbed in my own proposals, and ignored him; but there are people whom that trick with the hat might have put off completely. However, when I am thoroughly worked up I disregard not only such annoyances as these, but everything. I see, it is true, all that is going on, but do not admit it, so to speak, to my consciousness until I am finished, or until some objection has been raised. Thus I noticed quite well, for instance, that N. was by no means in a receptive state; holding on to the arms of his chair, he twisted about uncomfortably, never even glanced up at me, but gazed blankly, as if searching for something, into vacancy, and his face was so impassive that one might have thought no syllable of what I was saying, indeed no awareness of my presence, had penetrated to him.

Yes, his whole bearing, the bearing of a sick man, in itself inauspicious for me, I took in quite well; nevertheless I talked on as if I had still some prospect of putting everything right again by my talk, by the advantageous offers I made—I was myself alarmed by the concessions I granted, concessions that had not even been asked for. It gave me a certain satisfaction also to notice that the agent, as I verified by a fleeting glance, had at last left his hat in peace and folded his arms across his chest; my performance, which was partly, I must confess, intended for him, seemed to have given a severe blow to his designs. And in the elation produced by this result I might perhaps have gone on talking for a long time still, if the son, whom until now I had regarded as a secondary factor in my plans, had not suddenly raised himself in his bed and pulled me up by shaking his fist. Obviously he wanted to say something, to point out something, but he had not strength enough. At first I thought that his mind was wandering, but when I involuntarily glanced at old N. I understood better.

N. sat with wide-open, glassy, bulging eyes, which seemed on the point of failing; he was trembling and his body was bent forward as if someone were holding him down or striking him on the shoulders; his lower lip, indeed the lower jaw itself with the exposed gums, hung down helplessly; his whole face seemed out of joint; he still breathed, though with difficulty; but then, as if released, he fell back against the back of his chair, closed his eyes, the mark of some great strain passed over his face and vanished, and all was over. I sprang to him and seized his lifeless hand, which was so cold that it sent a chill through me; no pulse beat there now. So it was all over. Still, he was a very old man. We would be fortunate if we all had such an easy death. But how much there was to be done! And what should one do first? I looked around for help; but the son had drawn the bedclothes over his head, and I could hear his wild sobbing; the agent, cold as a fish, sat immovably on his chair, two steps from N., and was obviously resolved to do nothing, to wait for what time would bring; so I, only I was left to do something, and the hardest thing that anyone could be asked to do, that was to tell the news to his wife in some bearable form, in a form that did not exist, in other words. And already I could hear her eager shuffling steps in the next room.

Still wearing her outdoor clothes—she had not found time to change—she brought in a nightshirt that she had warmed before the fire for her husband to put on. "He's fallen asleep," she said, smiling and shaking her head, when she found us sitting so still. And with the infinite trustfulness of the innocent she took up the same hand that I had held a moment before with such fear and repugnance, kissed it playfully, and—how could we three others have borne the sight?—N. moved, yawned loudly, allowed his nightshirt to be put on, endured with a mixture of annoyance and irony his wife's tender reproaches for having overstrained himself by taking such a long walk, and strangely enough said in reply, to provide no doubt a different explanation for his having fallen asleep, something about feeling bored. Then, so as not to catch cold by going through the draughty passage into a different room, he lay down for the time being in his son's bed; his head was bedded down beside his son's feet on two cushions hastily brought by his wife. After all that had gone before I found nothing particularly odd in that. Then he asked for the evening paper, opened it without paying any attention to his guests, but did not read it, only glancing through it here and there, and made several very unpleasant observations on our offers, observations which showed astonishing shrewdness, while he waved his free hand disdainfully, and by clicking his tongue indicated that our business methods had left a bad taste in his mouth. The agent could not refrain from making one or two untimely remarks, no doubt he felt in his insensitive way that some compensation was due to him after what had happened, but his way of securing it was the worst he could have chosen. I said goodbye as soon as I could, I felt almost grateful to the agent; if he had not been there I would not have had the resolution to leave so soon.

In the lobby I met Frau N. again. At the sight of that pathetic figure I said impulsively that she reminded me a little of my mother. And as she remained silent I added: "Whatever people say, she could do wonders. Things that we destroyed she could make whole again. I lost her when I was still a child." I had spoken with deliberate slowness and distinctness, for I assumed the old lady was hard of hearing. But she must have been quite deaf, for she asked without transition: "And how does my husband look to you?" From a few parting words I noticed, moreover, that she confused me with the agent; I like to think that otherwise she would have been more forthcoming.

Then I descended the stairs: The descent was more tiring than the ascent had been, and not even that had been easy. Oh, how many business calls come to nothing, and yet one must keep going.

MY NEIGHBOR

MY BUSINESS rests entirely on my own shoulders. Two girl clerks with typewriters and ledgers in the anteroom, my own room with writing desk, safe, consulting table, easy chair, and telephone: such is my entire working apparatus. So simple to control, so easy to direct. I'm quite young, and lots of business comes my way. I don't complain, I don't complain.

At the beginning of the year a young man snapped up the empty premises next to mine, which very foolishly I had hesitated to rent until it was too late. They also consist of a room and an anteroom, with a kitchen, however, thrown in —the room and anteroom I would certainly have found some use for, my two girl clerks feel somewhat overdriven as it is— but what use would a kitchen have been to me? This petty consideration was solely responsible for my allowing the premises to be snatched from under my nose. Now that young man sits there. Harras, his name is. What he actually does there I have no idea. On the door is a sign: "Harras Bureau." I have made inquiries and I am told it is a business similar to mine. One can't exactly warn people against extending the fellow credit, for after all he is a young and pushing man who probably has a future; yet one can't go so far as to advise it, for by all appearances he has no assets yet. The usual thing said by people who don't know.

127

Sometimes I meet Harras on the stairs; he seems always to be in an extraordinary hurry, for he literally shoots past me. I have never got a good look at him yet, for his office key is always in his hand when he passes me. In a trice he has the door open. Like the tail of a rat he has slipped through and I'm left standing again before the sign "Harras Bureau," which I have read already far oftener than it deserves.

The wretchedly thin walls betray the honorable and capable man, but shield the dishonest. My telephone is fixed to the wall that separates me from my neighbor. But I single that out merely as a particularly ironical circumstance. For even if it hung on the opposite wall, everything could be heard in the next room. I have accustomed myself to refrain from naming the names of my customers when speaking on the telephone to them. But of course it does not need much skill to guess the names from characteristic but unavoidable turns of the conversation. Sometimes I absolutely dance with apprehension around the telephone, the receiver at my ear, and yet can't help divulging secrets.

Because of all this my business decisions have naturally become unsure, my voice nervous. What is Harras doing while I am telephoning? If I wanted to exaggerate—and one must often do that so as to make things clear in one's mind—I might assert that Harras does not require a telephone, he uses mine, he pushes his sofa against the wall and listens; while I at the other side must fly to the telephone, listen to all the requests of my customers, come to difficult and grave decisions, carry out long calculations—but worst of all, during all this time, involuntarily give Harras valuable information through the wall.

Perhaps he doesn't wait even for the end of the conversation, but gets up at the point where the matter has become clear to him, flies through the town with his usual haste and, before I have hung up the receiver, is already at his goal working against me.

A COMMON CONFUSION

A COMMON EXPERIENCE, resulting in a common confusion. A has to transact important business with B in H. He goes to H for a preliminary interview, accomplishes the journey there in ten minutes, and the journey back in the same time, and on returning boasts to his family of his expedition. Next day he goes again to H, this time to settle his business finally. As that by all appearances will require several hours, A leaves very early in the morning. But although all the surrounding circumstances, at least in A's estimation, are exactly the same as the day before, this time it takes him ten hours to reach H. When he arrives there quite exhausted in the evening he is informed that B, annoyed at his absence, had left half an hour before to go to A's village, and that they must have passed each other on the road. A is advised to wait. But in his anxiety about his business he sets off at once and hurries home.

This time he covers the distance, without paying any particular attention to the fact, practically in an instant. At home he learns that B had arrived quite early, immediately after A's departure, indeed that he had met A on the threshold and reminded him of his business; but A had replied that he had no time to spare, he must go at once.

In spite of this incomprehensible behavior of A, however,

B had stayed on to wait for A's return. It is true, he had asked several times whether A was not back yet, but he was still sitting up in A's room. Overjoyed at the opportunity of seeing B at once and explaining everything to him, A rushes upstairs. He is almost at the top, when he stumbles, twists a sinew, and almost fainting with the pain, incapable even of uttering a cry, only able to moan faintly in the darkness, he hears B—impossible to tell whether at a great distance or quite near him—stamping down the stairs in a violent rage and vanishing for good.

THE BRIDGE

I WAS STIFF AND COLD, I was a bridge, I lay over a ravine. My toes on one side, my fingers clutching the other, I had clamped myself fast into the crumbling clay. The tails of my coat fluttered at my sides. Far below brawled the icy trout stream. No tourist strayed to this impassable height, the bridge was not yet traced on any map. So I lay and waited; I could only wait. Without falling, no bridge, once spanned, can cease to be a bridge.

It was towards evening one day—was it the first, was it the thousandth? I cannot tell—my thoughts were always in confusion and perpetually moving in a circle. It was towards evening in summer, the roar of the stream had grown deeper, when I heard the sound of a human step! To me, to me. Straighten yourself, bridge, make ready, railless beams, to hold up the passenger entrusted to you. If his steps are uncertain steady them unobtrusively, but if he stumbles show what you are made of and like a mountain god hurl him across to land.

He came, he tapped me with the iron point of his stick, then he lifted my coattails with it and put them in order upon me. He plunged the point of his stick into my bushy hair and let it lie there for a long time, forgetting me no doubt while he wildly gazed around him. But then—I was just following

131

him in thought over mountain and valley—he jumped with both feet on the middle of my body. I shuddered with wild pain, not knowing what was happening. Who was it? A child? A dream? A wayfarer? A suicide? A tempter? A destroyer? And I turned around so as to see him. A bridge to turn around! I had not yet turned quite around when I already began to fall, I fell and in a moment I was torn and transpierced by the sharp rocks which had always gazed up at me so peacefully from the rushing water.

THE BUCKET RIDER

COAL ALL SPENT; the bucket empty; the shovel useless; the stove breathing out cold; the room freezing; the trees outside the window rigid, covered with rime; the sky a silver shield against anyone who looks for help from it. I must have coal; I cannot freeze to death; behind me is the pitiless stove, before me the pitiless sky, so I must ride out between them and on my journey seek aid from the coaldealer. But he has already grown deaf to ordinary appeals; I must prove irrefutably to him that I have not a single grain of coal left, and that he means to me the very sun in the firmament. I must approach like a beggar, who, with the death rattle already in his throat, insists on dying on the doorstep, and to whom the cook accordingly decides to give the dregs of the coffeepot; just so must the coaldealer, filled with rage, but acknowledging the command "Thou shalt not kill," fling a shovelful of coal into my bucket.

My mode of arrival must decide the matter; so I ride off on the bucket. Seated on the bucket, my hands on the handle, the simplest kind of bridle, I propel myself with difficulty down the stairs; but once downstairs my bucket ascends, superbly, superbly; camels humbly squatting on the ground do not rise with more dignity, shaking themselves under the sticks of their drivers. Through the hard frozen streets we go at a regular

133

canter; often I am upraised as high as the first storey of a house; never do I sink as low as the house doors. And at last I float at an extraordinary height above the vaulted cellar of the dealer, whom I see far below crouching over his table, where he is writing; he has opened the door to let out the excessive heat.

"Coaldealer!" I cry in a voice burned hollow by the frost and muffled in the cloud made by my breath, "please, coaldealer, give me a little coal. My bucket is so light that I can ride on it. Be kind. When I can I'll pay you."

The dealer puts his hand to his ear. "Do I hear right?" he throws the question over his shoulder to his wife. "Do I hear right? A customer."

"I hear nothing," says his wife, breathing in and out peacefully while she knits on, her back pleasantly warmed by the heat.

"Oh yes, you must hear," I cry. "It's me; an old customer; faithful and true; only without means at the moment."

"Wife," says the dealer, "it's someone, it must be; my ears can't have deceived me so much as that; it must be an old, a very old customer, that can move me so deeply."

"What ails you, man?" says his wife, ceasing from her work for a moment and pressing her knitting to her bosom. "It's nobody, the street is empty, all our customers are provided for; we could close down the shop for several days and take a rest."

"But I'm sitting up here on the bucket," I cry, and numb frozen tears dim my eyes, "please look up here, just once; you'll see me directly; I beg you, just a shovelful; and if you give me more it'll make me so happy that I won't know what to do. All the other customers are provided for. Oh, if I could only hear the coal clattering into the bucket!"

"I'm coming," says the coaldealer, and on his short legs he makes to climb the steps of the cellar, but his wife is already beside him, holds him back by the arm and says: "You stay here; seeing you persist in your fancies I'll go myself. Think of the bad fit of coughing you had during the night. But for a piece of business, even if it's one you've only fancied in your head, you're prepared to forget your wife and child and sacrifice your lungs. I'll go."

"Then be sure to tell him all the kinds of coal we have in stock! I'll shout out the prices after you."

"Right," says his wife, climbing up to the street. Naturally she sees me at once. "Frau Coaldealer," I cry, "my humblest greetings; just one shovelful of coal; here in my bucket; I'll carry it home myself. One shovelful of the worst you have. I'll pay you in full for it, of course, but not just now, not just now." What a knell-like sound the words "not just now" have, and how bewilderingly they mingle with the evening chimes that fall from the church steeple nearby!

"Well, what does he want?" shouts the dealer. "Nothing," his wife shouts back, "there's nothing here; I see nothing, I hear nothing; only six striking, and now we must shut up the shop. The cold is terrible; tomorrow we'll likely have lots to do again."

She sees nothing and hears nothing; but all the same she loosens her apron strings and waves her apron to waft me away. She succeeds, unluckily. My bucket has all the virtues of a good steed except powers of resistance, which it has not; it is too light; a woman's apron can make it fly through the air.

"You bad woman!" I shout back, while she, turning into the shop, half contemptuous, half reassured, flourishes her fist in the air. "You bad woman! I begged you for a shovelful of the worst coal and you would not give it me." And with that I ascend into the regions of the ice mountains and am lost forever.

A CROSSBREED

I HAVE a curious animal, half kitten, half lamb. It is a legacy from my father. But it only developed in my time; formerly it was far more lamb than kitten. Now it is both in about equal parts. From the cat it takes its head and claws, from the lamb its size and shape; from both its eyes, which are wild and flickering, its hair, which is soft, lying close to its body, its movements, which partake both of skipping and slinking. Lying on the window sill in the sun it curls up in a ball and purrs; out in the meadow it rushes about like mad and is scarcely to be caught. It flees from cats and makes to attack lambs. On moonlight nights its favorite promenade is along the eaves. It cannot mew and it loathes rats. Beside the hen coop it can lie for hours in ambush, but it has never yet seized an opportunity for murder.

I feed it on milk; that seems to suit it best. In long draughts it sucks the milk in through its fang-like teeth. Naturally it is a great source of entertainment for children. Sunday morning is the visiting hour. I sit with the little beast on my knees, and the children of the whole neighborhood stand around me.

Then the strangest questions are asked, which no human being could answer: Why there is only one such animal, why I rather than anybody else should own it, whether there was

ever an animal like it before and what would happen if it
died, whether it feels lonely, why it has no children, what it
is called, etc.

I never trouble to answer, but confine myself without further
explanation to exhibiting my possession. Sometimes the children bring cats with them; once they actually brought two
lambs. But against all their hopes there was no scene of recognition. The animals gazed calmly at each other with their
animal eyes, and obviously accepted their reciprocal existence
as a divine fact.

Sitting on my knees, the beast knows neither fear nor lust
of pursuit. Pressed against me it is happiest. It remains faithful
to the family that brought it up. In that there is certainly no
extraordinary mark of fidelity, but merely the true instinct of
an animal which, though it has countless step-relations in the
world, has perhaps not a single blood relation, and to which
consequently the protection it has found with us is sacred.

Sometimes I cannot help laughing when it sniffs around
me and winds itself between my legs and simply will not be
parted from me. Not content with being lamb and cat, it almost insists on being a dog as well. Once when, as may happen to anyone, I could see no way out of my business problems
and all that they involved, and was ready to let everything go,
and in this mood was lying in my rocking chair in my room,
the beast on my knees, I happened to glance down and saw
tears dropping from its huge whiskers. Were they mine, or
were they the animal's? Had this cat, along with the soul of a
lamb, the ambitions of a human being? I did not inherit much
from my father, but this legacy is quite remarkable.

It has the restlessness of both beasts, that of the cat and
that of the lamb, diverse as they are. For that reason its skin
feels too tight for it. Sometimes it jumps up on the armchair
beside me, plants its front legs on my shoulder, and puts its
muzzle to my ear. It is as if it were saying something to me,
and as a matter of fact it turns its head afterwards and gazes

in my face to see the impression its communication has made.
And to oblige it I behave as if I had understood, and nod.
Then it jumps to the floor and dances about with joy.

Perhaps the knife of the butcher would be a release for
this animal; but as it is a legacy I must deny it that. So it
must wait until the breath voluntarily leaves its body, even
though it sometimes gazes at me with a look of human understanding, challenging me to do the thing of which both of us
are thinking.

THE KNOCK AT THE
MANOR GATE

IT WAS SUMMER, a hot day. With my sister I was passing the
gate of a great house on our way home. I cannot tell now
whether she knocked on the gate out of mischief or out of
absence of mind, or merely threatened it with her fist and did
not knock at all. A hundred paces further on along the road,
which here turned to the left, began the village. We did not
know it very well, but no sooner had we passed the first house
when people appeared and made friendly or warning signs to
us; they were themselves apparently terrified, bowed down with
terror. They pointed towards the manor house that we had
passed and reminded us of the knock on the gate. The proprietor of the manor would charge us with it, the interrogation
would begin immediately. I remained quite calm and also tried
to calm my sister's fears. Probably she had not struck the
door at all, and if she had, nowhere in the world would that
be a reason for prosecution. I tried to make this clear to the
people around us; they listened to me but refrained from
passing any opinion. Later they told me that not only my
sister, but I too, as her brother, would be charged. I nodded
and smiled. We all gazed back at the manor, as one watches
a distant smoke cloud and waits for the flames to appear. And
right enough we presently saw horsemen riding in through the

wide-open gate. Dust rose, concealing everything, only the tops of the tall spears glittered. And hardly had the troop vanished into the manor courtyard before they seemed to have turned their horses again, for they were already on their way to us. I urged my sister to leave me, I myself would set everything right. She refused to leave me. I told her that she should at least change, so as to appear in better clothes before these gentlemen. At last she obeyed and set out on the long road to our home. Already the horsemen were beside us, and even before dismounting they inquired after my sister. She wasn't here at the moment, was the apprehensive reply, but she would come later. The answer was received almost with indifference; the important thing seemed their having found me. The chief members of the party appeared to be a young lively fellow, who was a judge, and his silent assistant, who was called Assmann. I was asked to enter the farmhouse. Shaking my head and hitching up my trousers, I slowly began to move, while the sharp eyes of the party scrutinized me. I still half believed that a word would be enough to free me, a city man, and with honor too, from this peasant folk. But when I had stepped over the threshold of the parlor the judge, who had hastened in front and was already awaiting me, said: "I'm really sorry for this man." And it was beyond all possibility of doubt that by this he did not mean my present state, but something that was to happen to me. The room looked more like a prison cell than the parlor of a farmhouse. Great stone flags on the floor, dark, quite bare walls, into one of which an iron ring was fixed, in the middle something that looked half a pallet, half an operating table.

Could I still endure any other air than prison air? That is the great question, or rather it would be if I still had any prospect of release.

THE CITY COAT OF ARMS

AT FIRST all the arrangements for building the Tower of Babel were characterized by fairly good order; indeed the order was perhaps too perfect, too much thought was given to guides, interpreters, accommodations for the workmen and roads of communication, as if there were centuries before one to do the work in. In fact, the general opinion at that time was that one simply could not build too slowly; a very little insistence on this would have sufficed to make one hesitate to lay the foundations at all. People argued in this way: The essential thing in the whole business is the idea of building a tower that will reach to heaven. In comparison with that idea everything else is secondary. The idea, once seized in its magnitude, can never vanish again; so long as there are men on the earth there will be also the irresistible desire to complete the building. That being so, however, one need have no anxiety about the future; on the contrary, human knowledge is increasing, the art of building has made progress and will make further progress, a piece of work which takes us a year may perhaps be done in half the time in another hundred years, and better done, too, more enduringly. So why exert oneself to the extreme limit of one's present powers? There would be some sense in doing that only if it were likely that the tower could be completed in one generation. But that is beyond all hope. It is far more likely that the next generation with their perfected knowledge will find the work of their predecessors bad, and tear down what has been built so as to begin anew. Such thoughts paralyzed people's powers, and so they troubled less about the tower than the construction of a city for the workmen. Every nationality wanted the finest quarter for itself, and this gave rise to disputes, which developed into bloody conflicts. These conflicts never came to an end; to the leaders they were a new proof that, in the absence of the necessary unity, the building of the tower must be done very slowly, or indeed preferably postponed until universal peace was declared. But the time was spent not only in conflict; the town was embellished in the intervals, and this unfortunately enough evoked fresh envy and fresh conflict. In this fashion the age of the first generation went past, but none of the succeeding ones showed any difference; except that technical skill increased and with it occasion for conflict. To this must be added that the second or third generation had already recognized the senselessness of building a heaven-reaching tower; but by that time everybody was too deeply involved to leave the city.

All the legends and songs that came to birth in that city are filled with longing for a prophesied day when the city would be destroyed by five successive blows from a gigantic fist. It is for that reason too that the city has a closed fist on its coat of arms.

THE SILENCE OF
THE SIRENS

PROOF that inadequate, even childish measures may serve to rescue one from peril:

To protect himself from the Sirens Ulysses stopped his ears with wax and had himself bound to the mast of his ship. Naturally any and every traveler before him could have done the same, except those whom the Sirens allured even from a great distance; but it was known to all the world that such things were of no help whatever. The song of the Sirens could pierce through everything, and the longing of those they seduced would have broken far stronger bonds than chains and masts. But Ulysses did not think of that, although he had probably heard of it. He trusted absolutely to his handful of wax and his fathom of chain, and in innocent elation over his little stratagem sailed out to meet the Sirens.

Now the Sirens have a still more fatal weapon than their song, namely their silence. And though admittedly such a thing has never happened, still it is conceivable that someone might possibly have escaped from their singing; but from their silence certainly never. Against the feeling of having triumphed over them by one's own strength, and the consequent exaltation that bears down everything before it, no earthly powers can resist.

And when Ulysses approached them the potent songstresses actually did not sing, whether because they thought that this enemy could be vanquished only by their silence, or because the look of bliss on the face of Ulysses, who was thinking of nothing but his wax and his chains, made them forget their singing.

But Ulysses, if one may so express it, did not hear their silence; he thought they were singing and that he alone did not hear them. For a fleeting moment he saw their throats rising and falling, their breasts lifting, their eyes filled with tears, their lips half parted, but believed that these were accompaniments to the airs which died unheard around him. Soon, however, all this faded from his sight as he fixed his gaze on the distance, the Sirens literally vanished before his resolution, and at the very moment when they were nearest to him he knew of them no longer.

But they—lovelier than ever—stretched their necks and turned, let their awesome hair flutter free in the wind, and freely stretched their claws on the rocks. They no longer had any desire to allure; all that they wanted was to hold as long as they could the radiance that fell from Ulysses' great eyes.

If the Sirens had possessed consciousness they would have been annihilated at that moment. But they remained as they had been; all that had happened was that Ulysses had escaped them.

A codicil to the foregoing has also been handed down. Ulysses, it is said, was so full of guile, was such a fox, that not even the goddess of fate could pierce his armor. Perhaps he had really noticed, although here the human understanding is beyond its depths, that the Sirens were silent, and held up to them and to the gods the afore-mentioned pretense merely as a sort of shield.

PROMETHEUS

THERE ARE FOUR LEGENDS concerning Prometheus:

According to the first he was clamped to a rock in the Caucasus for betraying the secrets of the gods to men, and the gods sent eagles to feed on his liver, which was perpetually renewed.

According to the second Prometheus, goaded by the pain of the tearing beaks, pressed himself deeper and deeper into the rock until he became one with it.

According to the third his treachery was forgotten in the course of thousands of years, forgotten by the gods, the eagles, forgotten by himself.

According to the fourth everyone grew weary of the meaningless affair. The gods grew weary, the eagles grew weary, the wound closed wearily.

There remained the inexplicable mass of rock. The legend tried to explain the inexplicable. As it came out of a substratum of truth it had in turn to end in the inexplicable.

THE TRUTH ABOUT
SANCHO PANZA

WITHOUT MAKING any boast of it Sancho Panza succeeded in
the course of years, by feeding him a great number of romances
of chivalry and adventure in the evening and night hours, in
so diverting from himself his demon, whom he later called
Don Quixote, that this demon thereupon set out, uninhibited,
on the maddest exploits, which, however, for the lack of a
pre-ordained object, which should have been Sancho Panza
himself, harmed nobody. A free man, Sancho Panza phil-
osophically followed Don Quixote on his crusades, perhaps
out of a sense of responsibility, and had of them a great and
edifying entertainment to the end of his days.

THE PROBLEM OF OUR LAWS

OUR LAWS are not generally known; they are kept secret by the small group of nobles who rule us. We are convinced that these ancient laws are scrupulously administered; nevertheless it is an extremely painful thing to be ruled by laws that one does not know. I am not thinking of possible discrepancies that may arise in the interpretation of the laws, or of the disadvantages involved when only a few and not the whole people are allowed to have a say in their interpretation. These disadvantages are perhaps of no great importance. For the laws are very ancient; their interpretation has been the work of centuries, and has itself doubtless acquired the status of law; and though there is still a possible freedom of interpretation left, it has now become very restricted. Moreover the nobles have obviously no cause to be influenced in their interpretation by personal interests inimical to us, for the laws were made to the advantage of the nobles from the very beginning, they themselves stand above the laws, and that seems to be why the laws were entrusted exclusively into their hands. Of course, there is wisdom in that—who doubts the wisdom of the ancient laws?—but also hardship for us; probably that is unavoidable.

The very existence of these laws, however, is at most a mat-

147

ter of presumption. There is a tradition that they exist and that they are a mystery confided to the nobility, but it is not and cannot be more than a mere tradition sanctioned by age, for the essence of a secret code is that it should remain a mystery. Some of us among the people have attentively scrutinized the doings of the nobility since the earliest times and possess records made by our forefathers—records which we have conscientiously continued—and claim to recognize amid the countless number of facts certain main tendencies which permit of this or that historical formulation; but when in accordance with these scrupulously tested and logically ordered conclusions we seek to adjust ourselves somewhat for the present or the future, everything becomes uncertain, and our work seems only an intellectual game, for perhaps these laws that we are trying to unravel do not exist at all. There is a small party who are actually of this opinion and who try to show that, if any law exists, it can only be this: The Law is whatever the nobles do. This party see everywhere only the arbitrary acts of the nobility, and reject the popular tradition, which according to them possesses only certain trifling and incidental advantages that do not offset its heavy drawbacks, for it gives the people a false, deceptive and over-confident security in confronting coming events. This cannot be gainsaid, but the overwhelming majority of our people account for it by the fact that the tradition is far from complete and must be more fully inquired into, that the material available, prodigious as it looks, is still too meager, and that several centuries will have to pass before it becomes really adequate. This view, so comfortless as far as the present is concerned, is lightened only by the belief that a time will eventually come when the tradition and our research into it will jointly reach their conclusion, and as it were gain a breathing space, when everything will have become clear, the law will belong to the people, and the nobility will vanish. This is not maintained in any spirit of hatred against the nobility; not at all, and by no one. We are more inclined to hate ourselves, because we have not yet shown ourselves worthy of being entrusted with the laws. And that is the real reason why the party who believe that there is no law have remained so few—although their doctrine is in certain ways so attractive, for it unequivocally recognizes the nobility and its right to go on existing.

Actually one can express the problem only in a sort of paradox: Any party which would repudiate, not only all belief in the laws, but the nobility as well, would have the whole people behind it; yet no such party can come into existence, for nobody would dare to repudiate the nobility. We live on this razor's edge. A writer once summed the matter up in this way: The sole visible and indubitable law that is imposed upon us is the nobility, and must we ourselves deprive ourselves of that one law?

ON PARABLES

MANY COMPLAIN that the words of the wise are always merely parables and of no use in daily life, which is the only life we have. When the sage says: "Go over," he does not mean that we should cross to some actual place, which we could do anyhow if the labor were worth it; he means some fabulous yonder, something unknown to us, something that he cannot designate more precisely either, and therefore cannot help us here in the very least. All these parables really set out to say merely that the incomprehensible is incomprehensible, and we know that already. But the cares we have to struggle with every day: that is a different matter.

Concerning this a man once said: Why such reluctance? If you only followed the parables you yourselves would become parables and with that rid of all your daily cares.

Another said: I bet that is also a parable.

The first said: You have won.

The second said: But unfortunately only in parable.

The first said: No, in reality: in parable you have lost.

A LITTLE FABLE

"ALAS," said the mouse, "the world is growing smaller every day. At the beginning it was so big that I was afraid, I kept running and running, and I was glad when at last I saw walls far away to the right and left, but these long walls have narrowed so quickly that I am in the last chamber already, and there in the corner stands the trap that I must run into." "You only need to change your direction," said the cat, and ate it up.

"HE"

NOTES FROM THE YEAR 1920

HE IS never quite ready for any contingency, yet he cannot even blame himself for that, for when in this life, which insists so mercilessly that we must be ready at every moment, can one ever find time in which to make oneself ready? and even if there were time how can one make ready before knowing the task; in other words, can one ever be equal to a natural task, a spontaneous task that has not merely been artificially concocted? So he has long since fallen under the wheels; a contingency for which, strangely enough, but also comfortingly enough, he was least ready of all.

All that he does seems to him, it is true, extraordinarily new, but also, because of the incredible spate of new things, extraordinarily amateurish, indeed scarcely tolerable, incapable of becoming history, breaking short the chain of the generations, cutting off for the first time at its most profound source the music of the world, which before him could at least be divined. Sometimes in his arrogance he has more anxiety for the world than for himself.

153

He could have resigned himself to a prison. To end as a prisoner—that could be a life's ambition. But it was a barred cage that he was in. Calmly and insolently, as if at home, the din of the world streamed out and in through the bars, the prisoner was really free, he could take part in everything, nothing that went on outside escaped him, he could simply have left the cage, the bars were yards apart, he was not even a prisoner.

He has the feeling that merely by being alive he is blocking his own way. From this sense of hindrance, in turn, he deduces the proof that he is alive.

The bony structure of his own forehead blocks his way; he batters himself bloody against his own forehead.

He feels imprisoned on this earth, he feels constricted; the melancholy, the impotence, the sicknesses, the feverish fancies of the captive afflict him; no comfort can comfort him, since it is merely comfort, gentle head-splitting comfort glozing the brutal fact of imprisonment. But if he is asked what he actually wants he cannot reply, for—that is one of his strongest proofs—he has no conception of freedom.

Some deny the existence of misery by pointing to the sun; he denies the existence of the sun by pointing to misery.

The sluggish, self-torturing, wavelike motion of all life, whether of other life or his own, which often seems to stagnate for a long time but in reality never ceases, tortures him because it brings with it the never-ceasing compulsion to think. Sometimes it seems to him that this torture heralds events. When he hears that a friend is awaiting the birth of a child he recognizes that in thought he has already suffered for that birth.

He sees in two ways: the first is a calm contemplation, consideration, investigation, an overflow of life inevitably involving a certain sensation of comfort. The possible manifestations of this process are infinite, for though even a woodlouse needs a relatively large crevice in which to accommodate itself, no space whatever is required for such labors; even where not the smallest crack can be found they may exist in tens of thousands, mutually interpenetrating one another. That is the first stage. The second is the moment when he is called upon to render an account of all this, finds himself incapable of uttering a sound, is flung back again on contemplation, etc., but now, knowing the hopelessness of it, can no longer dabble about in it, and so makes his body heavy and sinks with a curse.

This is the problem: Many years ago I sat one day, in a sad enough mood, on the slopes of the Laurenziberg. I went over the wishes that I wanted to realize in life. I found that the most important or the most delightful was the wish to attain a view of life (and—this was necessarily bound up with it—to convince others of it in writing), in which life, while still retaining its natural full-bodied rise and fall, would simultaneously be recognized no less clearly as a nothing, a dream, a dim hovering. A beautiful wish, perhaps, if I had wished it rightly. Considered as a wish, somewhat as if one were to hammer together a table with painful and methodical technical efficiency, and simultaneously do nothing at all, and not in such a way that people could say: "Hammering a table together is nothing to him," but rather, "Hammering a table together is really hammering a table together to him, but at the same time it is nothing," whereby certainly the hammering would have become still bolder, still surer, still more real and, if you will, still more senseless.

But he could not wish in this fashion, for his wish was not a wish, but only a vindication of nothingness, a justification of non-entity, a touch of animation which he wanted to lend to non-entity, in which at that time he had scarcely taken his first few conscious steps, but which he already felt as his element. It was a sort of farewell that he took from the illusive world of youth; although youth had never directly deceived him, but only caused him to be deceived by the utterances of all the authorities he had around him. So is explained the necessity of his "wish."

He proves nothing but himself, his sole proof is himself, all his opponents overcome him at once but not by refuting him (he is irrefutable), but by proving themselves.

Human associations rest on this, that someone by superior force of life gives the appearance of having refuted other individuals in themselves irrefutable. The result is sweet and comforting for those individuals, but it is deficient in truth and invariably therefore in permanence.

He was once part of a monumental group. Around some elevated figure or other in the center were ranged in carefully thought-out order symbolical images of the military caste, the arts, the sciences, the handicrafts. He was one of those many figures. Now the group is long since dispersed, or at least he has left it and makes his way through life alone. He no longer has even his old vocation, indeed he has actually forgotten what he once represented. Probably it is this very forgetting that gives rise to a certain melancholy, uncertainty, unrest, a certain longing for vanished ages, darkening the present. And yet this longing is an essential element in human effort, perhaps indeed human effort itself.

He does not live for the sake of his personal life; he does not think for the sake of his personal thoughts. It seems to

him that he lives and thinks under the compulsion of a
family, which, it is true, is itself superabundant in life and
thought, but for which he constitutes, in obedience to some
law unknown to him, a formal necessity. Because of this unknown family and this unknown law he cannot be exempted.

The original sin, the ancient wrong committed by man,
consists in the complaint, which man makes and never ceases
making, that a wrong has been done to him, that the original sin was once committed upon him.

Two children were loitering beside Casinelli's shop window,
a boy of about six, a girl of seven, both well dressed; they
were talking of God and sin. I stopped behind them. The
girl, who seemed to be a Catholic, held that the only real
sin was to deceive God. With childish obstinacy the boy,
who seemed to be a Protestant, asked what, then, it was to
deceive human beings or to steal. "That's a very great sin
too," said the girl "but not the greatest, the greatest sins are
those against God; for sins against human beings we have the
confessional. When I confess the angel again stands behind
me in an instant, for when I commit a sin the devil comes
behind me, only I don't see him." And tired of being half in
earnest, she spun around light-heartedly on her heel and said:
"Look, there's nobody behind me." The boy spun around too
and saw me there. "Look," he said, without considering that
I must hear him, or perhaps without caring, "the devil is
standing behind me." "I see him too," replied the girl, "but
that's not the one I meant."

He does not want consolation, yet not because he does not
want it—who does not want it?—but because to seek for
consolation would mean to devote his whole life to the task,
to live perpetually on the very frontiers of his existence, al-

most outside it, barely knowing for whom he was seeking consolation, and consequently not even capable of finding effective consolation, effective, not real consolation, for real consolation does not exist.

He fights against having his limits defined by his fellow men. No man, even if he be infallible, can see more than that fraction of his neighbor for which his strength and kind of vision are adapted. He has, however, like everybody, but in its most extreme form, the longing to limit himself to the limit of his neighbor's eyesight. Had Robinson Crusoe never left the highest, or, more correctly, the most visible point of his island, from desire for comfort, or timidity, or fear, or ignorance, or longing, he would soon have perished; but since without paying any attention to passing ships and their feeble telescopes he started to explore the whole island and take pleasure in it, he managed to keep himself alive and finally was found after all, by a chain of causality that was, of course, logically inevitable.

"You make a virtue of your necessity."
"In the first place everyone does that, and in the second, that's just what I don't do. I let my necessity remain necessity. I do not drain the swamp, but live in its feverish exhalations."
"That's the very thing you make a virtue of."
"Like everyone, as I said before. But I only do it for your sake. I take injury to my soul that you may remain friendly to me."

Everything is allowed him, except self-oblivion, wherewith, however, everything in turn is denied him, except the one thing necessary at the given moment for the whole.

The question of conscience is a social imposition. All virtues are individual, all vices social. The things that pass as social virtues, love, for example, disinterestedness, justice, self-sacrifice, are only "astonishingly" enfeebled social vices.

The difference between the "Yes" and "No" that he says to his contemporaries and those that he should actually say, might be likened to the difference between life and death, and is just as vaguely divined by him.

The reason why posterity's judgment of individuals is juster than the contemporary one lies in their being dead. One develops in one's own style only after death, only when one is alone. Death is to the individual like Saturday evening to the chimney sweep; it washes the dirt from his body. Then it can be seen whether his contemporaries harmed him more, or whether he did the more harm to his contemporaries; in the latter case he was a great man.

The strength to deny, that most natural expression of the perpetually changing, renewing, dying, reviving human fighting organism, we possess always, but not the courage, although life is denial, and therefore denial affirmation.

He does not die along with his dying thoughts. Dying is merely a phenomenon within the inner world (which remains intact, even if it too should be only an idea), a natural phenomenon like any other, neither happy nor sad.

The current against which he swims is so rapid that in certain absent moods he is sometimes cast into despair by the blank peace amid which he splashes, so infinitely far has he been driven back in a moment of surrender.

He is thirsty, and is cut off from a spring by a mere clump of bushes. But he is divided against himself: one part overlooks the whole, sees that he is standing here and that the spring is just beside him; but another part notices nothing, has at most a divination that the first part sees all. But as he notices nothing he cannot drink.

He is neither bold nor rash. But neither is he fearful. A free life would not alarm him. Now he has never been granted such a life, but that too causes him no anxiety, for he has no anxiety of any kind about himself. There exists, however, a Someone completely unknown to him, who has a great and continuous anxiety for him—for him alone. This anxiety of this Someone concerning him, and in particular the continuousness of this anxiety, sometimes causes him torturing headaches in his quieter hours.

A certain heaviness, a feeling of being secured against every vicissitude, the vague assurance of a bed prepared for him and belonging to him alone, keeps him from getting up; but he is kept from lying still by an unrest which drives him from his bed, by his conscience, the endless beating of his heart, the fear of death and the longing to refute it: all this will not let him rest and he gets up again. This up and down and a few fortuitous, desultory, irrelevant observations made in the course of it, are his life.

He has two antagonists: The first pushes him from behind, from his origin. The second blocks his road ahead. He struggles with both. Actually the first supports him in his struggle with the second, for the first wants to push him forward; and in the same way the second supports him in his struggle with the first; for the second of course forces him back. But it is only theoretically so. For it is not only the two protagonists

who are there, but he himself as well, and who really knows
his intentions? However that may be, he has a dream that
sometime in an unguarded moment—it would require, though,
a night as dark as no night has ever been—he will spring out
of the fighting line and be promoted, on account of his experience of such warfare, as judge over his struggling antagonists.

REFLECTIONS ON
SIN, PAIN, HOPE, AND
THE TRUE WAY[1]

1

THE TRUE WAY goes over a rope which is not stretched at any great height but just above the ground. It seems more designed to make people stumble than to be walked upon.

2

All human error is impatience, a premature renunciation of method, a delusive pinning down of a delusion.

3

There are two cardinal sins from which all the others spring: impatience and laziness. Because of impatience we were driven out of Paradise, because of laziness we cannot return. Perhaps, however, there is only one cardinal sin: im-

---

[1] These aphorisms were carefully written out and numbered by Kafka himself on separate pieces of paper. Where two aphorisms have the same number they are written on the same sheet of paper. Those marked with an asterisk were crossed out by Kafka, but not removed from their place in the sequence.

patience. Because of impatience we were driven out, because of impatience we cannot return.

4

Many of the shades of the departed occupy themselves with nothing but sipping the waves of the river of death, for it comes from us and still has the salt savor of our seas. Then the river turns in its loathing, flows backward, and sweeps the dead into life again. They, however, are overjoyed, chant songs of thanksgiving, and caress the indignant stream.

5

From a certain point onward there is no longer any turning back. That is the point that must be reached.

6

The decisive moment in human development is a continuous one. For this reason the revolutionary movements which declare everything before them to be null and void are in the right, for nothing has yet happened.

7*

One of the Evil One's most effectual arts of seduction is the challenge to battle. It is like the fight with woman, which ends in bed.

8

A is greatly puffed up, he believes that he has made vast progress in virtue, since, apparently because he is a more challenging figure, he finds more and more temptations assailing him from directions hitherto unknown to him. The real explanation, however, is that a more powerful devil has taken possession of him, and that the host of smaller devils have run to serve the greater.

9

The diversity of ideas which one can have, say, of an apple: the apple as it appears to the child who must stretch his neck so as barely to see it on the table, and the apple as it appears to the master of the house who picks it up and lordly hands it to his guest.

10

A first sign of nascent knowledge is the desire for death. This life seems unendurable, any other unattainable. One is no longer ashamed of wishing to die; one prays to be conducted from the old cell that one hates into a new one that one has yet to hate. There is in this a vestige of faith that during the change the Master may chance to walk along the corridor, contemplate the prisoner, and say: "You must not lock up this one again. He is to come to me."

11*

If you were walking over a plain with the honest desire to make progress, and yet found yourself further back than when you started, then it would be a hopeless business; but as you are clambering up a steep precipice, as steep, say, as you yourself seen from below, your backward slips may only be caused after all by the lie of the land, and you must not despair.

12

Like a road in autumn: Hardly is it swept clean before it is covered again with dead leaves.

13

A cage went in search of a bird.

14

I have never been in this place before. One breathes differently, a new star near the sun shines more blindingly than the sun.

15

If it had been possible to build the Tower of Babel without ascending it, the work would have been permitted.

16*

Do not let the Evil One persuade you that you can have any secrets from him.

17

Leopards break into the temple and drink the sacrificial chalices dry; this occurs repeatedly, again and again: finally it can be reckoned upon beforehand and becomes a part of the ceremony.

18

As firmly as the hand grips the stone. But the hand's grip is firm merely that it may fling the stone the farther. Yet the road leads also to that far place where the stone falls.

19

You are the problem. No scholar to be found far and wide.

20

From a real antagonist boundless courage flows into you.

21

Grasp your great good fortune that the ground on which you stand cannot be greater than the two feet that cover it.

22

How can one be glad of the world, unless one is flying to it for refuge?

23*

There are countless places of refuge, there is only one place of salvation; but the possibilities of salvation, again, are as numerous as all the places of refuge.

There is a goal, but no way; what we call the way is only wavering.

24

What is laid upon us is to accomplish the negative; the positive is already given.

25

Once we have granted accommodation to the Evil One he no longer demands that we should believe him.

26

The afterthoughts with which you justify your accommodation of the Evil One are not yours but those of the Evil One.

The animal snatches the whip from its master and whips itself so as to become master, and does not know that all this is only a fantasy caused by a new knot in the master's whiplash.

27*

Virtue is in a certain sense disconsolate.

28

I do not strive for self-command. Self-command signifies the will to operate at a certain fortuitous point in the endless radiations of my spiritual existence. But if I must draw such circles around me, then I will do it better by remaining passive in simple astonishment at the tremendous complex, and will take away with me nothing but the strengthening power which that spectacle gives by contrast.

29

The crows maintain that a single crow could destroy the heavens. Doubtless that is so, but it proves nothing against the heavens, for the heavens signify simply: the impossibility of crows.

30

The martyrs do not underestimate the body; they cause it to be elevated on the cross. In that they are at one with their enemies.

31

His weariness is that of the gladiator after the combat; his work was the whitewashing of a corner in a state official's office.

32

There is no having, only being, only a being panting for its last breath, panting to be choked out.

33

Formerly I could not understand why I received no answer to my questions; today I cannot understand how I could have believed I could question. But indeed I did not believe, I simply questioned.

34

His reply to the assertion that he *possesses* perhaps, but never *is*, was only a trembling and pounding of the heart.

35

A man was astonished how easily he went the eternal way; he happened to be rushing backwards along it.

36

One cannot pay the Evil One in installments—and yet one perpetually tries to do it.

It is conceivable that Alexander the Great, in spite of the martial successes of his early days, in spite of the excellent army that he had trained, in spite of the power he felt within him to change the world, might have remained standing on the bank of the Hellespont and never have crossed it, and not out of fear, not out of indecision, not out of infirmity of will, but because of the mere weight of his own body.

37*

The road is endless, there is nothing that can be subtracted from it or added to it, and yet everyone insists on applying his own childish measuring yard. "Yes, you will have to go the length of that measuring yard as well; it will not be for given you."

38*

Only our concept of Time makes it possible for us to speak of the Day of Judgment by that name; in reality it is a summary court in perpetual session.

39*

The disharmony of the world seems, comfortingly enough, to be merely an arithmetical one.

40

Let the face that is filled with loathing and hate sink on your breast.

41

The hunting dogs are still playing in the courtyard, but the hare will not escape them, no matter how fast it may already be flying through the woods.

42

You have harnessed yourself ridiculously for this world.

43

The more horses you yoke the quicker everything will go— not the rending of the block from its foundation, which is impossible, but the snapping of the traces and with that the gay and empty journey.

44

The word *"sein"* signifies in German both things: to be, and to belong to Him.

45

The choice was put to them whether they would like to be kings or king's couriers. Like children they all wanted to be couriers. So now there are a great many couriers, they post through the world, and, as there are no kings left, shout to each other their meaningless and obsolete messages. They would gladly put an end to their wretched lives, but they dare not because of their oath of service.

46

Faith in progress does not mean faith that progress has already been made. That would be no faith.

47

A is a virtuoso and the heavens are his witness.

48*

Man cannot live without an enduring trust in something indestructible in himself. Yet while doing that he may all his life be unaware of that indestructible thing and of his trust in it. One of the possible ways in which this permanent unawareness may be expressed is to have faith in a personal God.

49*

The mediation of the serpent was necessary: Evil can seduce men, but it cannot become man.

50*

In the fight between you and the world back the world.

51

One must not cheat anybody, not even the world of its triumph.

52

There is only a spiritual world; what we call the physical world is the evil in the spiritual one, and what we call evil is only a necessary moment in our endless development.

In a light that is fierce and strong one can see the world dissolve. To weak eyes it becomes solid, to weaker eyes it shows fists, before still weaker eyes it feels ashamed and smites down him who dares to look at it.

53

All is deception: one can try to live with the minimum of illusion, take things as they are, or try to live with the maximum of illusion. In the first case one betrays good by wanting to make its achievement too easy, and evil by imposing overwhelmingly unfavorable fighting conditions upon it. In the second case one betrays good by refusing to strive towards it even on the earthly plane. In the third case one betrays good by sundering oneself as far as possible from it, and evil by hoping that through its ubiquity it may be rendered innocuous. From this it seems that the second course is the one to be preferred, for in every case one betrays good, but in this case one does not betray evil, at least in appearance.

54

There are questions which we could never get over if we were not delivered from them by the operation of nature.

55

For all things outside the physical world language can be employed only as a sort of adumbration, but never with even approximate exactitude, since in accordance with the physical world it treats only of possession and its connotations.

56*

A man lies as little as he can only when he lies as little as he can, not when he is given the smallest possible opportunity to lie.

57*

A flight of steps which has not been hollowed out by many feet is, from its own point of view, only a blank wooden contraption that has been hammered together.

58

He who renounces the world must love all men, for he renounces their world too. He begins from that point to divine the true nature of mankind, which cannot but be loved, providing that one is capable of it.

59*

If you love your neighbor within the world you do no more and no less injustice than in loving yourself within the world. The only question that remains is whether the first is possible.

60

The fact that there is only a spiritual world robs us of hope and gives us certainty.

61

Our art is a dazzled blindness before the truth: The light on the grotesque recoiling phiz is true, but nothing else.

62

The expulsion from Paradise is in its main significance eternal: Consequently the expulsion from Paradise is final, and life in this world irrevocable, but the eternal nature of the occurrence (or, temporally expressed, the eternal recapitulation of the occurrence) makes it nevertheless possible that not only could we live continuously in Paradise, but that we are continuously there in actual fact, no matter whether we know it here or not.

63

He is a free and secure citizen of the world, for he is fettered to a chain which is long enough to give him the freedom of all earthly space, and yet only so long that nothing can drag him past the frontiers of the world. But simultaneously he is a free and secure citizen of Heaven as well, for he is also fettered by a similarly designed heavenly chain. So that if he heads, say, for the earth, his heavenly collar throttles him, and if he heads for Heaven, his earthly one does the same. And yet all the possibilities are his, and he feels it;

more, he actually refuses to account for the deadlock by an error in the original fettering.

64

He rushes after facts like a novice on skates, a novice, moreover, who is practicing in a place where it is forbidden to skate.

65

What can be a greater source of happiness than belief in a household god!

66

Theoretically there exists a perfect possibility of happiness: to believe in the indestructible element in oneself and not strive after it.

67

The indestructible is one; it is every human being individually and at the same time all human beings collectively; hence the marvelous indissoluble alliance of mankind.

68*

There exist in the same human being varying perceptions of one and the same object which differ so completely from each other that one can only deduce the existence of different subjects in the same human being.

69

He eats the droppings from his own table; thus he manages to stuff himself fuller than the others for a little, but meanwhile he forgets how to eat from the table; thus in time even the droppings cease to fall.

70

If that which is supposed to have been destroyed in Paradise was destructible, then it was not decisive; but if it was indestructible, then we are living in a false belief.

71

Test yourself on humanity. It makes the doubtful doubt, the believer believe.

72

That feeling: "Here I must not anchor"—and immediately afterwards to feel the raging, rushing stream on every side of you!

A revulsion. Watching, fearing, hoping, the answer steals around the question, peers despairingly in her enigmatic face, follows her through the maddest paths, that is the paths leading farthest away from the answer.

73

Intercourse with human beings seduces one to self-contemplation.

74

The spirit only becomes free when it ceases to be a prop.

75

Profane love can seem more sublime than sacred love; of itself it could not do this, but as, unknown to itself, it possesses an element of sacred love, it can.

76*

Truth is indivisible, therefore cannot know itself; the man who desires to know it must be false.

77

No one can desire what is fundamentally harmful to him. If individuals seem to do so—and perhaps they always seem to do so—that can be explained by the fact that in every apparently individual being there is one self desiring something which in fact is beneficial to that self but very harmful to a second self, who is called more or less to sit in judgment on the case. If the human being had taken the side of this second self from the very beginning, and not after the case was judged, the first self would have been annulled, and the desire along with him.

78

Why do we lament over the fall of man? We were not driven out of Paradise because of it, but because of the Tree of Life, that we might not eat of it.

79

We are sinful not merely because we have eaten of the Tree of Knowledge, but also because we have not yet eaten of the Tree of Life. The state in which we find ourselves is sinful, quite independent of guilt.

80

We were fashioned to live in Paradise, and Paradise was destined to serve us. Our destiny has been altered; that this has also happened with the destiny of Paradise is not stated.

81

Evil is a radiation of the human consciousness at certain transitional stages. The physical world itself is not really an illusion, but only its evil, which, however, admittedly constitutes our picture of the physical world.

82

Since the Fall we have been essentially equal in our capacity to recognize good and evil; none the less it is just here that we seek to show our individual superiority. But the real differences of worth begin beyond that knowledge. The opposite illusion may be explained thus: nobody can remain content with the mere knowledge of good and evil in itself, but must endeavor as well to act in accordance with it. The strength to do so, however, is not likewise given him, consequently he must destroy himself trying to do so, at the risk of not achieving the necessary strength even then; yet there remains nothing for him but this final attempt. (That is moreover the meaning of the threat of death attached to eating of the Tree of Knowledge; perhaps too it was the original meaning of natural death.) Now, faced with this attempt, man is filled with fear; he prefers to annul his knowledge of good and evil (the term, "the fall of man," may be traced back to that fear); yet the accomplished cannot be annulled, but only confused. It was for this purpose that our rationalizations were created. The whole world is full of them, indeed the whole visible world is perhaps nothing more than the rationalization of a man who wants to find peace for a moment. An attempt to falsify the actuality of knowledge, to regard knowledge as a goal still to be reached.

83

A faith like a guillotine, as heavy, as light.

84

Death confronts us not unlike the historical battle scene that hangs on the wall of the classroom. It is our task to obscure or quite obliterate the picture by our deeds while we are still in this world.

85

A man has freedom of will and a threefold freedom at that: Firstly, he was free when he willed this life; now, it is true, he cannot cancel that fact, for he is no longer the same man who once willed it, except insofar as he is carrying out, by the act of living, what he once willed.

Secondly, he is free in that he can choose the road he is to take in this life and the manner in which he is to walk it.

Thirdly, he is free in that, as an entity which he will some time be again, he has the desire to go through life no matter what happens and so eventually find himself, following a path which, though he can choose it, is yet so labyrinthine that it leaves not a single inch of this life untouched.

This is the threefold aspect of the freedom of the will, but it is also, being simultaneous, a unity, and at bottom so completely a unity that it leaves no room for a will, neither for a free nor for an unfree one.

86*

Two possibilities: to make oneself, or to be infinitesimally small. The second is fulfillment, therefore inaction, the first a beginning, therefore action.

87*

To avoid an error in the use of words: What is to be deliberately destroyed must first have been quite soundly conserved; what crumbles, crumbles, but cannot be destroyed.

88

The original worship of idols certainly arose from a fear of things, but that involved a fear of the necessity of things, and with that a fear of one's responsibility for things. So vast seemed this responsibility that man did not even dare to lay it on a single superhuman being; for by the mediation of one being human responsibility would not still have been lightened enough, intercourse with only one being would still have been far too deeply tinged with responsibility; so man endowed every thing with responsibility for itself, more, he endowed every thing also with a limited responsibility for man.

89*

For the last time psychology!

90*

Two tasks on the threshold of life: To narrow your circle more and more, and constantly to make certain that you have not hidden yourself somewhere outside it.

91*

Evil is often like a tool in one's hand; knowingly or unknowingly it will allow itself to be laid aside without protest, if one only has the will.

92

The joys of this life are not its own, but our dread of ascending to a higher life; the torments of this life are not its own, but our self-torment because of that dread.

93

Only here is suffering suffering. Not in the sense that those who suffer here are ennobled somewhere else because of their suffering, but in the sense that what is called suffering in this world is, without any alteration, except that it is freed from its opposite, bliss in another.

94

One's idea of the infinite extent and fullness of the cosmos is the reward of a combination of laborious creation and perfectly detached self-consciousness, both pushed to their uttermost extremes.

95

How much more crushing than the most pitiless conviction of our present sinful state is even the feeblest conviction that there will be eternal justification for our temporal existence. Only our strength in supporting this second conviction, which in its purity completely subsumes the first, is the measure of faith.

Some people assume that in addition to the great original betrayal a small particular betrayal has been contrived in every case exclusively for them, that, in other words, when a love drama is being performed on the stage the leading actress has not only a pretended smile for her lover, but also a special crafty smile for one particular spectator at the back of the gallery. That is going too far.

96

Knowledge of the diabolical there can be, but not belief in it, for anything more diabolical than that could not exist.

97

Sin always comes openly, and can be grasped at once by the senses. It comes root and all, and does not have to be torn up.

98

We too must suffer all the suffering around us. What each of us possesses is not a body but a process of growth, and it conducts us through every pain, in this form or in that. Just as the child unfolds through all the stages of life to old age and death (and every stage seems unattainable to the previous one, whether in fear or longing) so we unfold (not less deeply bound to humanity than to ourselves) through all the sufferings of this world. In this process there is no place for justice, but no place either for dread of suffering or for the interpretation of suffering as a merit.

99

You can hold back from the suffering of the world, you have free permission to do so and it is in accordance with your nature, but perhaps this very holding back is the one suffering that you could have avoided.

100

The means this world employs to seduce us, and the seal of the warrant that this world is only a passing stage, are one and the same. Rightly so, for only thus could this world seduce us, and besides it squares with the truth. The worst of it, however, is that after being successfully seduced we forget the warrant and so find ourselves tempted by good into evil, tempted by woman's eyes into her bed.

101

Humility provides everyone, even the lonely and despairing, with the firmest relation to his fellow men, a relation, too, that is instantaneous, though only if the humility is complete and permanent. It can do this because it is the true language of prayer, at once worship and firmest union. Our relation to our fellow men is that of prayer, our relation to ourselves, that of effort; from prayer we draw the strength for effort.

Can you know anything but illusion? If once illusion were destroyed you would never dare to look back; you would be turned into a pillar of salt.

102

Everybody feels very kindly towards A, somewhat as one solicitously guards an excellent billiard table even from passable players, until the great player arrives, carefully examines the cloth, refuses to countenance the slightest defect, but then, when he himself begins to play, gives free and pitiless vent to his fury.

103

"But then he returned to his work as if nothing had happened." That is a saying which sounds familiar to us from an indefinite number of old tales, though in fact it perhaps occurs in none.

104

"No one can say that we are wanting in faith. The mere fact of our living is itself inexhaustible in its proof of faith."

"You call that a proof of faith? But one simply cannot not live."

"In that very 'simply cannot' lies the insane power of faith; in that denial it embodies itself."

You do not need to leave your room. Remain sitting at your table and listen. Do not even listen, simply wait. Do not even wait, be quite still and solitary. The world will freely offer itself to you to be unmasked, it has no choice, it will roll in ecstasy at your feet.